LIQUID
DECEPTIONS

LIQUID DECEPTIONS
Copyright © 2022 by Colleen Hlavac
All rights reserved

ISBN: 979-8-9853697-1-7

See more at:
www.colleenhlavac.com

LIQUID DECEPTIONS

COLLEEN HOFSTADTER HLAVAC

For my husband, Mark, who has always supported and provided guidance with my writing endeavors.

1

"I have a confession to make and I can only tell you. You might want to sit down for this. It started many years ago. Tiny hints of it were already there in my childhood and it only continued to worsen. Come closer. I am going to need to whisper this in your ear. I will die if anyone overhears me. You can never tell another living soul. It will be in your best interest to keep quiet.

I used to have dark thoughts, very dark thoughts. They were like a constant companion to me in my childhood, kind of like an imaginary friend. I even named them Kevin. My thoughts then graduated into actions. Well, here's the thing, remember how Sis died in that drowning accident years ago? Her death fascinated me…"

He had been stalking her for almost seventeen months, studying her every move, her patterns, her mannerisms and habits. He was essentially an expert on her life. Heck, he knew her better than her own mother did. He was a virtuoso in Tinsley Banks. The thought humored him and made him chuckle. He knew that Honey Nut Cheerios ranked among her favorite cereals and that her closest friends were Roseanne, Melissa and Peter. She had a weakness for nachos topped with grilled chicken and drinks garnished with lime. Tinsley frequently spent time with her friends at the neighborhood Mexican restaurant. Watching them through the windows of the establishment provided him with hours of award winning entertainment. The Academy Awards were a snooze fest compared to tuning in to this vixen's life.

He was one of Tinsley's 2,793 Facebook friends. She was the foolish kind, an attention hungry woman who accepted any random friend request. He made sure to never message her or like any of her posts. He was smarter than that. Someday soon, her lifeless body would be found and the last thing he wanted was to have any sort of obvious ties to her. The hunger to kill her was reaching a boiling point. He had been very patient. How much longer could he hold off on the inevitable? He did not have the answer to that question. Realizing that the time to murder was rapidly approaching calmed his frayed nerves.

2

"Bang! Boom! Pop!" Despite using ear protection, the sound of gunfire blared in Cosette DuPont's ears. She was in the final days of her twenty-four week Police Academy Training in Carson City, Nevada. Currently, her class was heavily engrossed in their hostage simulation. During the assignment, the instructors regularly complimented Cosette on her lightning quick reflexes. She figured she may have developed this trait since she was lucky enough to have had her young son, Spencer. As a mom, she was required to be alert and energetic every day of the year, 24/7.

This career was a complete turn around from her former profession. She had previously been a flight attendant. Tragically, during her time at the airline, Cosette had become front and center of a murderous nightmare. Her best friend, Maggie, was brutally slain by a local serial killer. He wreaked havoc on the small town of Virginia City, Nevada. In fact, she, herself, had been kidnapped by him and had almost become one of his many murder victims. She still suffered from regular night terrors because of what she had endured.

Had it not been for the bravery and determination of local law enforcement and, of course, her beloved fiancé, Luke Meier, she would certainly no longer be among the living. The mere thought sent shivers up and down Cosette's spine.

Losing her best friend and having a front row seat to the destruction serial killers have on so many people's lives, allowed her to realize that she had developed a passion for catching and bringing criminals to justice. Her fiancé and Cosette's mother, Evelyn, were very supportive of her career aspirations. They both helped care for her five year old son while she was away at training.

Cosette was one of twenty-six people in her police academy program. She was the only woman in the class. When the academy began, she felt intimidated. Although her height was a statuesque 5'8", she was delicately built and small boned. The men in her class were very respectful and kind to her. In fact, Gary and Tommy had become two of her best friends. They supported each other and served as each other's sounding boards during the grueling training. They timed each other as they raced along the academy's track and cheered each other on when they were doing pull-ups and sit-ups.

She missed Spencer and Luke every minute of every day. However, Cosette made the most of her weekends off during training. Her doting fiancé whisked her and Spencer away to his stunning cabin on the shores of Lake Tahoe for the majority of her days off. They basked on the expansive deck of the home while Luke helped her study for any upcoming law enforcement tests. They enjoyed Luke's barbecues. The aroma of the rich, sweet smoke from the meats caused their mouths to water. After their meals, the couple usually dipped intermittently between the steaming hot tub and the frigid Tahoe water.

One evening, Luke and Spencer even took her on a sunset cruise. They embarked on their adventure with Luke's boat. The water was choppy. The strong wind blew across Emerald Bay and forced the waves to ripple. The wind driven waves delighted her son and he called out, "It is like we are on a roller coaster! Woo hee!"

Luke and Cosette chuckled at their darling Spencer's enthusiasm. The clouds above were painted in ever changing colors. From tangerine orange to a vivid, almost fluorescent pink, the sun was beginning its daily ritual. The sky developed into a darker red. It reminded Cosette of the rich, flavorful, crystal glass of Pinot Noir she was currently enjoying.

The radiant streaks in the sky cast a gleam onto the water. The clouds looked like great, burgundy colored wings.

Then, the most beautiful of all commenced; the art which was the night sky. Stars bedazzled the heavens and the moon demurely made its nightly debut. The full moon cast a warm, milky glow onto the lake and spilled over the rooftops of the local homes. It shone like a silvery orb. The cool air whipped Cosette's skin. She suppressed a shiver. She could see two sleepy looking coyotes wandering on a nearby beach. Since they were nocturnal animals, they clearly were just beginning to rouse from a deep slumber. The duo started to eerily yip and howl into the cold, night air. Cosette was fascinated and amused by the coyotes. Spencer cuddled up close to her as they watched the night life awaken.

Then, they begrudgingly decided to call it a night. Cosette had to get up early in the morning to return to the academy.

The trio docked the watercraft and disembarked. As they traversed the lawn, Luke noticed an out of place looking item nestled between the expansive lawn and the beginning of the ground cover. He reached down curiously and picked it up. "How odd! It's a wallet." He searched the contents. It was completely empty. Luke brought it into the brightly lit kitchen so he could inspect it more closely.

"This wallet is made of stingray skin."

"How would you know that, sweetheart?" inquired Cosette.

"I had a stingray skin wallet in my teens. I know the look and feel of it. Also, notice the design? On the front of the wallet is a white, elongated oval. That is commonly seen on stingray wallets."

"Hmm, strange it was on your property."

The fatigue of the day was catching up on all of them. They tucked Spencer into his bed. Then the couple cuddled all night in their cozy and serene bedroom. Cosette felt happier than she had ever been in her life. She was eager to start their wedding planning. She could barely wait to officially become Luke's wife. She needed to hold off with wedding preparations until she graduated from the police academy and became settled into her new job. Then the planning for their nuptials would begin. Cosette drifted off while protectively enveloped in Luke's strong arms.

3

Cosette walked down a dark, foreboding road in Virginia City. It was a crisp, wintry night. Against a gray sky, darkened branches appeared like demonic claws swaying above her. She heard the ravenous howls of wild dogs off in the distance. Suddenly, she detected insistent footsteps approaching her at the speed of a bullet train. Cosette quickened her pace but, to her horror, the footsteps sped up also. She started to sprint. The deafening sound of heavy footsteps raced behind her. All at once, calloused hands encircled her neck and the predator threw her barbarically onto the ground. She tried to scream but her lungs were unable to rummage for air. Finally, she was able to release a thunderous shriek.

She opened her eyes in horror and saw Luke looking at her intently and with a great deal of concern.

"Sweetheart, you were having another night terror. You are safe. You are at the lake house."

Cosette was drenched in sweat. She began to weep and Luke pulled her closer to him. He held her until she finally fell into a fitful sleep again.

Luke didn't say it but he had been very worried about his fiancée. She had night terrors often. Understandably, she was still traumatized by the former local serial killer. He was hoping that the gift of time and empowering herself by becoming a law enforcement officer would lessen her trauma and fear. He loved her more than it was possible for words to express. Cosette was everything to him. She was his world. He could not wait for the day that she would become his wife. He needed her and his mission in life was to always love and protect her.

The classmates were near the end of their training program. Excitement radiated amongst the students. Tommy, one of Cosette's closest friends at the academy, approached her with a proposition.

"As you know, my dad is head of the homicide detective division in Reno. Due to space issues at the police department, they are currently housing his unit in Virginia City. He said he can take on two new detectives, at this time. The Reno P.D. hired me and they would like you to work with us also. The Reno Police Department knows that you are at the top of our class. The job is yours if you are interested. Is there any way I could entice you to join us?"

Cosette was speechless. This was the job offer of her dreams. She longed to be a homicide detective. Generally, it took years of hard work to achieve this rank. Working as a beat cop did not appeal to her as much, although she had been fully prepared, of course, to put in the necessary time to reach her ultimate goal. The police department's offer of employment was a dream come true. She felt like she had to pinch herself. She got along very well with Tommy. She adored him. He was kind, fun and very loyal. Plus, they shared a similar work ethic. She had met his father, Frank Munro, on a few occasions already and she really enjoyed his company. He was a charming yet, down to earth man and he was a highly skilled detective. Additionally, Spencer and Cosette lived in a cottage in Virginia City. To actually be able to work in her own town was ideal. Her commute would consist of about three minutes of driving. She could even walk to work on days the weather permitted.

4

It was a festive Saturday night as Tinsley cheeringly clinked her glass of tequila against her friend, Peter's, margarita glass. Their favorite restaurant was nestled along the shores of South Lake Tahoe. Peter was an athletic, pleasant looking man with wheat colored, cropped hair, hazel eyes, and a powdering of freckles on his sun kissed face. Although he would be considered nice looking by most, he did not quite achieve the coveted ranks of hunk or pretty boy. As a child, he hated his freckles. The kids in school would tease him and say that it looked like someone had a mouth full of beige paint and spattered the contents at him. They roared in laughter at their recurrent joke while Peter blushed and cowered in the corner. His adoring mother would assure him that by the time he reached the age of eighteen, the pesky spots would magically vanish. Here he was, a decade after that age, and he still sported a face full of them. His parents were so intent on making him feel good about his freckles, that they even named their darling Shetland Sheepdog, Freckles, in hopes that Peter would connect the word to something positive. It made him feel better when Tinsley told him that his freckles were adorable and they gave his face the appearance of a tan year round. His pet Green-cheeked Conure, Pickles, was entertained by them for hours on end. She would peck at them in hopes that they would turn out to be bird seeds.

The establishment was packed full of lively customers tonight. Kitschy cacti and colorful parrot lights were pulsating throughout the room, adding to the jovial atmosphere. Peter and Tinsley had been friends since attending kindergarten together at Tahoe Valley Elementary school. They were both born and raised in the area. Their childhood summers were spent frolicking in the lake. During the winters they participated in the Squaw Valley Ski team. It was a beautiful place to grow up. At the age of twenty-eight they still had chosen not to move away from their picturesque hometown.

Both Tinsley and Peter were employed at the Crystal Waters Casino. It was the highest ranked and most trendy spot in town. Peter worked as a security guard and Tinsley was a cocktail waitress. She catered to the clients playing on the slot machines and the blackjack tables. Tinsley's warm personality and striking good looks ensured that she made a very comfortable salary on tips. Her bottled blond hair hit at the center of her back. She only stood at 5'5" but the majority of her height was due to her endlessly long, sleek legs. Her skin was a flawless, dewy canvas and her light green eyes were icy and mesmerized anyone who stared into their depths.

Tinsley sported a tiny dimple on her left cheek which only added to her charm. She was the type of woman who could drive fifty-five miles per hour in a school zone, have the crossing guard draped on her hood and she would still somehow manage to charm her way out of getting a speeding ticket.

Peter and Tinsley had embarked on a romantic relationship during the summer when they were twenty-two years old. Peter still remembered holding her in his arms and kissing her for what felt like eternity. Their days were spent basking on beaches under the Tahoe sun and kissing in the surf. At sunset, they usually enjoyed a picnic which included champagne and chocolate dipped strawberries, which they amorously fed to each other. Their nights were filled with intimacy and mind blowing passion. As the glorious summer turned into a crisp autumn, Tinsley decided that they were not meant to be anything more than friends. Peter was heartbroken and was dead set against her decision. In order to continue his friendship with her, Peter acted as if he completely agreed with the decision to terminate their romantic relationship. The truth was that he still pined and ached for her. He was deeply in love with her to this day, but he kept his feelings to himself. He would much rather continue a lifelong friendship with her than to have no ties left to her at all.

"Earth to Peter," stated Tinsley as she tapped her perfectly manicured, almond shaped, acrylic nails on the hardwood table top.

"You looked so lost in your thoughts. Is everything okay?"

Peter internally scolded himself for being distracted. He vowed that Tinsley could never learn that he was still hopelessly in love with her.

"Oh, I'm good. Sorry, I was just thinking about what a long shift I have at work tomorrow," fibbed Peter.

"Well, let's just enjoy the now. It is pretty early. You will still be able to get plenty of sleep before your shift."

"You're right, Tinsley."

They clinked their glasses again and drank from their bottomless drinks.

Both of their homes were just a few minutes walk from Casa Rosaria, their favorite restaurant. Their residences were in opposite directions but Peter always insisted on escorting

Tinsley directly to her door. He was very protective of her.

They exited into the gloom of the boulevard. Both felt sated and satisfied from their meals. The night sky was aglow with the bright lights from the local restaurants and stores. Tourists and locals whipped past them. Peter put his arm around Tinsley's shoulder as they strolled.

A man who appeared to be in his thirties approached them. Tinsley estimated that he was well over six feet tall. He had a shock of dark brown hair and his light eyes seemed to penetrate straight into her soul. He was leering at Tinsley. Something about him made her feel anxious. She shivered. Tinsley was generally a calm and trusting person. It was unusual for her to feel such fear. This man unnerved her. She let out a sigh of relief as he passed them without incident. She heard him whistle an eerie sounding tune.

Tinley's building was flanked between a candle making studio and an artisan coffee company. The coffee company was a small mom and pop shop. She preferred their coffee over the larger, more commercial companies, any day of the week. The scents in her home were abundant with the rich aroma of coffee beans and the fragrance of candles ranging from raspberries to eucalyptus.

Peter walked her directly to the front door. As they approached, Tinsley spotted something in an envelope on her door mat. "What's this?" inquired Tinsley. She opened the envelope. Inside, to her surprise, was a wallet. It felt buttery soft to the touch. It was black in color. On the front stood a white, oval shape design. The wallet was empty.

The couple looked at the object in a state of confusion.

"Did you order a wallet, Tinsley?"

"No, I just received a new one for my birthday. This is strange. Maybe someone left it at my door by accident. I will be on the lookout if anyone in the complex is missing a wallet. I can even post it on my Next-Door Neighbors' app."

"That is a good idea. Somebody is probably searching frantically for it," agreed her devoted friend.

Peter embraced her and wished her a good night's sleep.

Tinsley entered her townhouse. She was feeling jittery and she was unable to pinpoint why.

I didn't have a drop of coffee or tea all evening. I feel like I am on a caffeine high. I'm a wreck.

A single light burned on the kitchen table. It was her most recent purchase, a flameless rose scented candle. It illuminated the photographs of her family displayed on the walls. The photos conjured up so many sweet memories. Their shining faces managed to temporarily soothe her. Her mother always made everything better. If Tinsley was ever stressed or gloomy, her mother would make her a cup of camomile tea and take walks with her along a local river bank. The combination of the two activities worked wonders and made her feel better.

The large arched windows of the home allowed the street lights to filter into the room and illuminated Tinsley's toffee brown hardwood floors. On the coffee table, stood her favorite decor item, a succulent plant. It was nestled in an elephant planter. A dear friend had surprised her with the little gem. The elephant, and in particular, that its trunk was positioned in an upright position, symbolized good fortune. It always brightened her day to see it and added to the welcoming home environment which she strived for.

Tinsley startled when she spotted a figure. She scolded herself when she realized that it was simply her reflection in the gilded mirror she had received as a twenty-first birthday gift from her parents.

Why am I feeling so tense?

Tinsley heard water running from the upstairs bathroom. With her heart in her throat, she ran up the five steps into the guest bathroom. Indeed, the faucet was trickling. She never used this restroom. She only used the bathroom in the master bedroom. Chills danced up and down her spine. Had somebody been in here while she was at the restaurant? The thought to call Peter entered her mind.

Cut it out. You are being ridiculous, she scolded herself.

Tinsley removed her makeup, brushed her teeth and changed into her favorite pajamas, a violet, silk pant and top set. She slipped into bed. Her oversized, orange colored kitty, Putscho, had been waiting eagerly for her. He erupted into a chorus of satisfied purrs. The warmth from the feline's fur and his rhythmic whirs instantly relaxed Tinsley and she drifted off into a deep slumber.

Her morning alarm serenaded her with tropical bird calls. They chirped into her dreams and were the opening curtain call for her new day. The mid-morning sun poured into the window and glinted in Tinsley's eyes. It took her a moment to register that today was not a day off for her. She needed to report to the casino in an hour from now. Putscho pushed up against her, demanding his morning chin scratching. He made it very difficult for her to get out of bed and start her day.

Putscho was sixteen years old and Tinsley was extremely attached to him. She loved him as if he were her own baby. If it were up to Tinsley, she would spend this day, and every day, cuddling with her beloved pet and binge watching some of her favorite mystery shows. For as long as she could remember, her fantasy was to become a homicide detective. She knew that dream would never get fulfilled, so, at the very least, she could watch her detective shows and try to solve the crime before the narrator revealed the answer. That was the closest she was going to get to her aspirations.

Unfortunately, duty calls, she reminded herself and forced herself up and out of the bed in one swift movement.

5

Cosette's long awaited police academy graduation day had arrived. Her class assembled at the Douglas County Community Center.

The auditorium was packed full of guests. From her seat, Cosette, could see her mother, Luke, Spencer, Wyatt; Luke's cousin, and Austin; Luke's lifelong friend from Virginia City. Luke beamed with pride at his accomplished, dedicated fiancee.

Cosette was seated between her two dearest friends and fellow graduates, Tommy and Gary. Tommy warmly winked at her and gave her hand an encouraging squeeze during the ceremony. They both were in awe of the fact that today was finally their graduation day. The duo had worked tirelessly to reach the completion of the program.

The ceremony and after-party consisted of a whirlwind of activities. Cosette already knew that her fellow classmates were hard workers but they sure knew how to celebrate and let loose as well. It was an evening they would all never forget. Luke twirled her onto the dance floor. She felt heady from the combination of the champagne and the excitement about her accomplishment.

After the event, Cosette, Luke, and Spencer went to Luke's home which was situated high on a hilltop overlooking their beloved Virginia City. The mini celebration continued on the terrace of the backyard. Outdoor heaters ensured their comfort despite the frigid desert evening. In the darkness, Luke found Cosette and pulled her into his arms. Her entire body relaxed. The twinkling lights of the town below served as their muse for the night.

The golden illumination from the kitchens below glowed and dim street lanterns waved to them as if welcoming them home. The moon was a white-gold crescent and as the couple's eyes gazed heavenward, a blanket of stars which seemed to stretch to infinity, bloomed in the velvet black.

In the distance, a lonely owl called out. A Northern Mockingbird, a species known for having the ability to imitate the blaring of car alarms, was chirping in a nearby tree. A chilly breeze picked up and caused ripples in Luke's infinity pool.

Cosette then heard a familiar sound. "Co-coo-coo-coooo!"

"Is that who I think it is?" beamed Cosette.

"It sure is!" chuckled Luke.

It was Cosette's roadrunner, Romeo. She had missed him terribly while she had been away at the Police Academy. Romeo had been a regular visitor at Cosette's cottage in Virginia City. She had grown very attached to him. Unfortunately, he had injured himself and a local veterinarian felt it would be safer for him not to be released back into the desert. Luke and

Cosette had happily adopted him. He had become a treasured member of their family. He was even featured among the photos on last year's Christmas card. Romeo's excitement at being reunited with her was touching.

Cosette soaked in every minute of her life. She had everything she had ever wished for. She was engaged to the man of her dreams, had an adorable son, relished living in Virginia City and had just graduated from the police academy. Cosette's life had not always been this happy. In fact, she had endured a great deal of heartache in her past. She was married to Spencer's dad, Chad, for several years. It was a highly toxic relationship. Chad had never missed an opportunity to remind Cosette that she was worthless. He was cold and withdrawn throughout the majority of their marriage. It was painful when he finally filed for divorce. She had longed to keep the marriage going for the sake of their son. That option had been taken away from her. In retrospect, she knew that the demise of their marriage had ultimately been for the best. She had been able to rebuild her life and she was happier and more at peace now than she had been in her entire life. With that thought, she pulled Luke in extra close. She whispered in his ear, "Life is good." In the shadows of the garden, his face was so close to hers that she was able to detect the combination of his earthy aftershave and the whiskey sour they had just been enjoying. Their bodies pressed together and Cosette could feel their combined heartbeats. She closed her eyes and felt Luke's hand cross her body and finally rest on the back of her neck allowing him to pull her in even closer. Time stood still. Their lips trembled and met. It was a night the couple would not soon forget.

6

Tinsley gave herself an appraising glance in her full length mirror. She was ready to go to the casino. Her uniform consisted of a short, black skirt, red velvet off the shoulder top, fishnet stockings and three inch heels.

Assessing her skirt critically she thought,

If I didn't know better, I would think that the rest of my skirt is on layaway at the mall.

Tinsley was amazed and irritated that every year her uniform at the casino seemed to get even shorter and tighter.

She always wore her sterling silver necklace with a crescent moon pendant. Her face was fully made up and she even sported a pair of long, false eyelashes. Her lustrous hair had been blown dry and her straightening iron worked its magic. Tinsley knew she was a beautiful woman. She had heard it her entire life.

A lot of good that has done me, she thought bitterly.

My life is basically a dumpster fire. The only man I ever wanted dumped me and I have been in meaningless relationships ever since.

Soon after she had ended her relationship with Peter, Tinsley met Dawson. He was everything she had ever wanted in a man and she fell hopelessly in love with him. At least, she thought it was love at the time. Little did she know that while she was hinting to him what kind of engagement ring she would like him to give her, he got another girl pregnant and left Tinsley heartbroken and alone. She was devastated. He was now happily married to this lady and they had two beautiful children together. Just her luck!

Feeling moody and heavy hearted, Tinsley kissed Putscho goodbye, grabbed the Subaru keys and headed out into the glaring sunlight.

She arrived at the Crystal Waters Casino just seven minutes later. The buff and chronically friendly gate attendant, Tyler, greeted her warmly. "Well, good morning, beautiful. How are you today?"

"Better now!" flirted Tinsley while batting her endless eyelashes at him. He was clearly under her spell. He had been enthralled with her for years. The highlight of Tyler's shift was to get a glimpse of the enchanting Miss Tinsley Banks. She made his blood boil. After his shift, he would usually go and get a cocktail from her. It allowed him to interact with her one last time for the day. Her beauty was intimidating and he had not yet built up the nerve to ask her out on a date.

Tinsley whipped her car into the first space she found and sauntered into the casino. The heavy smell of cigar and cigarette smoke invaded her senses. Her eyes watered and the lingering, stale odors made her sneeze. The casino area was enshrouded in a hazy, gray fog due to the smoke in the air.

She clocked in and met up with two of her favorite cocktail waitresses, Roseanne and Melissa. They were both loyal friends and kind to the core. Melissa had over processed hair, soft gray eyes, tobacco stained, crooked teeth and a gaunt face from years of hard living. She was skinny and had the physique of a twelve year old boy until she had finally splurged and underwent breast implant surgery a couple of years ago. The surgeon was very generous with the size of implants he gave her. At times, it looked as if Melissa could topple over from the sheer weight of her chest.

Roseanne was a petite brunette with waist length, wavy hair and chocolate colored eyes which were full of emotion and softness. She always went above and beyond to help friends and coworkers and she possessed a fire cracker wit and a quick tongue which was ripe with sarcasm. Tinsley's friends made her shifts less grueling with their humor and entertaining stories.

"Girl, are we ever glad to see you. We have been slammed all morning. The hotel is booked solid with business conventions this week and these guests love to drink and gamble," complained Melissa.

"Oh well, at least the shift will seem to go faster," added Tinsley, already feeling weary.

Peter was on duty at the casino today as well. He regularly circulated through Tinsley's work area. As a security guard, he was assigned to monitor all areas of the casino's gaming area. It worked out beautifully that he could see Tinsley throughout his shift. It made his time there much more interesting.

A gentleman sat at one of the dollar slot machines and nursed his cocktail. The alluring Roseanne had just served him his first drink. He was positioned so he had the ultimate vantage point of Tinsley. By now, he had memorized her every curve and every expression. He zoomed in on her neck and felt an animal-like urge to attack her. He studied her delicate skin. A tiny mole positioned on the right side of her throat was particularly appealing. It reminded him of a target at a shooting range. When the day finally arrived, her neck would receive an abundance of his focus. He chuckled to himself at the delicious thought. In the meantime, he had always believed that enjoying an appetizer is essential before devouring any five star meal. His eyes shot back to Roseanne and a smile curled onto his face.

After Tinsley's shift had concluded, she met Peter, Roseanne and Melissa at the Neptune Swim Center located off of the Casino's pit. They had an afternoon together here at least twice a week. Tinsley changed into her skimpy, orange, polka dotted bikini. She strutted over to her usual long chaise and joined her awaiting friends. Moments later, Gabe Patterson, the handsome pool attendant served them their cocktails. He stood at 6'4" and had a well toned build. His jet black hair, olive green eyes and strong, square jaw only added to his captivating appearance. Tinsley, Roseanne and Melissa all perked up as he approached them. They flirted and giggled with him while Peter just rolled his eyes in annoyance. He was used to them fawning over this co-worker.

I mean, he's ok looking, thought Peter. *If you like that sort of thing!* Jealousy erupted within him.

Peter had to admit that Gabe was a pleasant and friendly man. It just didn't help his likability score that the woman he loved fawned all over him at every possible opportunity. He was surprised that Gabe had not asked Tinsley out yet. He thanked his lucky stars. It was rare for a man not to show interest in her.

7

It was Cosette's first day of work at the homicide detective unit. She parked in the poorly defined, gravel parking lot behind her new office and trudged up onto the mossy sidewalk. A wired fence bordered the property. The weed choked courtyard consisted of a small pond and potted succulents. A lonely Sierran Tree frog sat on the muddy bank. He made the sound, "ribbit", once as if to greet her on her first day of work.

I see a lot of potential here. A woman's touch will do wonders for this courtyard, thought Cosette excitedly.

She entered the building and was relieved to see Tommy's beaming face.

"Welcome to our first law enforcement job," Tommy gushed. Let me show you around the office. Dad should be back soon."

A dark walnut bookcase lined the entire right hand wall. The green curtain was faded and a tired looking potted palm was barely clinging to life. A calendar from 2010 featuring Rhodesian Ridgeback Dogs was tacked above Tommy's work space. It was opened to the month of May and featured an elegant looking dog sporting the distinctive ridge down her back. Tommy showed Cosette to her desk. It was next to the bay window and if she leaned a little to the right she was able to see the pond. Sunlight streamed through the beams of the courtyard.

Cosette's desk was solidly built and its surface was a glossy mahogany. It came complete with a brand new computer, a stapler and a charging station. The area was dimly lit since the only source of illumination was from an older, unshaded lamp. The light bulb flickered intermittently

Moments later, Tommy's father breezed into the office.

"Welcome and good morning, Cosette."

"Good morning, Mr Munro. I am very excited to be here."

"Please call me Frank. It is a pleasure to have you join our team."

Once the pleasantries were complete, the trio sat down for their first briefing.

"We have a client coming in today at 11:00 a.m. His name is Nicholas Trident. While our unit generally focusses on homicide cases, we do occasionally take on missing persons cases as well. Anyway, Nicholas had only been married for ten months when his bride suddenly disappeared. Law enforcement did some poking around and discovered that Amber Trident enjoyed the company of other men. They figured she up and left willingly since she had a habit of doing that a few times in her past. Nicholas doesn't buy their theory. He wants us to reevaluate and get to the bottom of what really happened. I'd love it if you could both sit in during my meeting with him. Cosette, I scheduled you to interview Amber's mom at her home in Carson City later this afternoon. Tommy, I would like you to interview one of Amber's exes, Jackson Herbert. He is willing to talk to us.

Jackson will come here, to our office, for an interview in a few hours. Nicholas needs closure. He is heartbroken and he will not be able to move forward with his life if he doesn't discover what really happened to his wife."

Cosette was jotting down all the pertinent facts. An excitement ignited within her. This would be her very first case. She would do everything in her power to uncover the truth for Mr. Trident.

8

Patsy Goodwin looked out of her bedroom window feeling weighed down by a deep sadness. Her husband, Jeff, had already left for work and she was all alone in their spacious home; a home which was supposed to be filled with their children. Their 3rd In-vitro-fertilization attempt had just failed. Patsy felt frustrated and anxious. She had longed to be a mother since she was in her early twenties. The couple had been married already for six years. They had attempted virtually every fertility treatment available. Sadly, they remained childless.

I need to go out and clear my head, thought Patsy.

She had the habit of taking a hike on her favorite trail at least once a week. She slipped into her leggings and a cheerful, yellow t-shirt with the words "Be happy" inscribed on the front. Finally, she donned her beige, suede hiking boots. She dabbed tinted sunscreen onto her tear streaked face.

At least make some effort with your appearance, she scolded herself.

I can't let myself go to pot just because our fertility treatments failed. Jeff isn't going to stay patient with my mood swings for much longer. I don't feel like adding divorce to my already sad life. Maybe this hike will cheer me up. Something is bound to alleviate my depression sooner or later.

One of Patsy's favorite aspects of living in South Lake Tahoe was that she had access to countless hiking trails. When they had first moved to the area, Patsy sampled a number of trails. She loved wandering through the Desolation Wilderness. The Glen Alpine Trail had quickly become her go to place to hike. At this time of day, she knew that she would have no trouble finding parking across the street from the trail at Lily Lake. She swept up her wavy, chestnut brown locks into a high ponytail and headed out the door to finally start her day. Five minutes later, she arrived at her destination and found the parking area to be empty.

Patsy started her trek. To her delight, she was far from alone. There was a chorus of Stellar's Jays serenading her in the crisp, morning air. She lifted her face and allowed the welcoming sunlight and gentle breeze to dance on her skin. Dragonflies whirred past her and dipped momentarily into the nearby stream. The woodsy smell was intoxicating."Splash!" A pinecone tumbled into the stream. The scattered clouds above blossomed into a light pink color as if trying to imitate the color of the striking wildflowers in the surrounding meadow. The lacy edged clouds rolled lazily across the blue sky and reminded Patsy of boats drifting aimlessly about in their celestial sea.

A waterfall was showcased along the trail. It was   sapphire blue in color and it drizzled softly into a varnish clear pool. The waterfall reminded Patsy of maple syrup running onto a fluffy stack of Belgian waffles, her favorite breakfast.

Patsy sighed. *Nature sure has a way of calming me and lifting my mood. This is exactly what I needed.*

Musty odors emanated from the surrounding redwood trees and river rocks.

He was there, monitoring her every move. The man had been watching her patterns and knew that she almost always walked here on Wednesdays during the mid-morning hours.

Patsy has been a very naughty girl. She disappointed me. I won't allow anyone to let me down. Patsy skipped her hike last Wednesday but, lo and behold, she made it for her hike today. People really are creatures of habit, so predictable. Sure, I lost a morning waiting for her here last week. That is okay because she was worth the wait, he reasoned.

The potential of their meet up kept him awake last night for hours on end. He felt like a child on Christmas morning. His entire body was electrified and overwhelmed with excitement and anticipation. Originally, it had been his intention to make Tinsley Banks his next victim. Plans had changed and she would be one of his eventual victims, but far from his next kill.

He rummaged into his trouser pocket to ensure that the Aquarius zodiac pendant was safe and sound. It would not count as a true murder for him if he failed to leave the little, silver trinket on the corpse.

I really need to stop being so OCD. I must have checked to make sure it was there about seventeen times in the last half hour. It is there, of course. Chill out, man.

He stayed about two hundred feet behind her and tip-toed, quieter than a church mouse, preparing to duck for cover, at all times, in case she turned around. He was dressed in earth tones from top to bottom in order to blend in with the backdrop.

She is so unaware of her surroundings. Don't these moms teach their daughters how to stay safe? Well, lucky for me, the average female is clueless, unaware and very easy to sneak up on. They make my work so easy, he thought with great amusement and he was forced to bite down on his sun damaged, chapped lips in order not to howl out loud with laughter. He had been rehearsing in his mind for days how he would approach her and how he would end her life.

After a final surveillance of the area, he felt confident that they were indeed alone. Approaching the intended victim from behind, and in a tone as sugary as the county faire cotton candy, he stated,

"Hello, Miss. I am sorry to bother you."

Patsy startled and jumped like a mountain goat scaling cliffs in the Swiss Alps.

"Oh my, I didn't see you there!" responded Patsy with a quivering voice.

"Sorry to startle you. I just have one question. Why would a pretty, young thing like you be stupid enough to walk alone on a trail? Didn't your mommy teach you anything?"

The monster roared in the most bone chilling laughter.

Patsy became overcome with dread. Her belly cramped violently and her hands became cold and clammy. Her skin blanched lighter than the shade of freshly plowed snow. Raw panic rose within her. Her legs felt wobbly. Her initial reaction was to step backwards and move away from the menacing figure but her shoes felt like they had weights on them. She tumbled over the root of a tree and fell onto the dusty ground.

As quick as a lightning strike, he positioned himself above her. His malicious scowl was just inches away from her face. His eyes were soulless and they were filled with greed and lust. Patsy could see the indescribable, sadistic pleasure he was receiving from attacking her.

He whipped his trusted rope from his pocket and wrapped the pre-tied noose around her neck. Patsy tried to fight him off but it was useless. He pulled the rope tightly and closed off her trachea. He had learned from past experience that if he let go of the pressure on the neck too early, his victim could regain consciousness. It was critical for him to continue to strangle for the duration of at least four to five minutes after the victim stopped struggling.

As he saw the life drain from her eyes, he began to feel increasingly alive. He was elated! The euphoria he was experiencing was earth shattering. He wished there was a way he could bottle this feeling but he knew the only way to duplicate the ecstasy was to kill again soon. The killer had waited months since his last slaying. He doubted he would be able to refrain from murdering that long this time.

He dragged Patsy's lifeless body down to the stream and positioned her next to the flowing water. It was critical for his enjoyment, that his victims get discarded near a body of water. It would feel incomplete for him otherwise.

Now, for the final touch, he pulled the necklace with the Aquarius pendant out and placed it below Patsy's bruised throat. It was a sparkling, sterling silver necklace with a round pendant depicting the Aquarius symbol, the Water Bearer. Below the symbol, the pendant stated the word, "Aquarius".

He then exited the trail system, whistling a bone chilling tune the entire way. The killer started fantasizing about the day that it would finally be time to end Tinsley's life.

9

Nicholas Trident came into the office right on time. He was relatively tall and very fit. Cosette noticed that he was the spitting image of the actor, David Beckham. Despite his good looks, he appeared disheveled and he sported dark circles under his eyes. He carried with him a distinct air of depression, even hopelessness.

Frank introduced him to Cosette and Tommy. Nicholas was an exceptionally kind and warm person despite the obvious pain he was dealing with. The four of them took a seat around a small pine table and the interview commenced. Frank did the majority of the speaking since he was much more seasoned in law enforcement. Their meeting lasted for over an hour and they were able to gain a great deal of information about Nicholas' missing bride.

Frank assured the gentleman that they would do everything in their power to uncover the truth about Amber's disappearance. Nicholas departed their office looking a little more hopeful and upbeat than when he had arrived.

Cosette went out to her car and followed the directions her GPS was giving her to Carson City. The drive gave her time to mull over and assess the details she had learned about Amber and her life. Cosette pulled up to a weather beaten, beige home at the far end of a quiet lane. The wood from the home's exterior had become silvered due to years of harsh sunlight. The only bright aspect to the home was a vibrant, ocean blue front door. The lawn was brown and patchy. The shingled roof appeared to be nearing the end of its life.

Cosette walked up the creaking steps and knocked gently on the front door.

A lady who appeared to be in her late sixties opened the door. Her gray hair was styled into a short, shapeless cut. Her eyes appeared lifeless and her skin was alarmingly pale, almost translucent.

"You must be Cosette DuPont?" the woman asked meekly. Before Cosette could respond, the lady continued,

"I'm Raquel, Amber's mother. Please come in."

"It is lovely meeting you, Raquel. I am eager to go over some information about your daughter," added Cosette politely.

Raquel walked with a slight limp into the family room. The scent of stale cigarettes mixed with vanilla scented air fresheners mingled in the air. A several month old, dried out Christmas tree was perched near the fireplace. The needles of the tired tree sloughed and coated the rug beneath. Three cats lounged along the patched up corduroy sofa. The tuxedo colored cat looked up at the ladies as they entered the room. He instantly lost interest in them and finally yawned and stretched lazily. Raquel motioned for Cosette to take a seat on the blue, wooden rocking chair. The wall next to the detective served as a kaleidoscope of family memories. Two young ladies were prominently displayed during different stages of their lives, ranging from babyhood, the teenage years and more recent portraits. Raquel noticed Cosette gazing at the wall.

"These are my two daughters. The one with the auburn hair is Amber. The brunette, Tricia, is the younger of the two. I love them both to the moon and back but my Tricia has never caused me an ounce of pain. I'm so proud of that girl."

Cosette looked at the stunning brunette's photos. Tricia looked self assured and her warm, toffee colored eyes were magnetic and brimming with genuine kindness and cheerfulness.

Raquel continued,"Tricia lives with her husband, Sam, in Florida. They have been blessed with seven children. She is the best mom. Tricia and Sam have always been deeply in love and supportive of each other. My daughter has a good life."

Raquel's face turned grey tinged and she suddenly looked somber.

"Unfortunately, my Amber is just the opposite of Tricia. She has had a very turbulent life. Sure, her heart is in the right place but drama and pain seem to follow her around. And now she is…gone."

The grieving mother's bloodshot eyes brimmed to capacity with tears.

"The cops keep insisting that she went away on her own, voluntarily. I don't believe their theory for a second."

Her pale face flashed with anger and despair.

"That is why I am here," Cosette assured. "The department asked us to revisit Amber's case. We will do everything possible to find answers for you and Amber's husband. Could you tell me more about your daughter? I hear that she has disappeared in the past without informing anyone about her whereabouts. Could you give me more details about those episodes?" prodded Cosette gently.

"Sure, she has left three times in the past seven years. All of the incidences happened before she met Nicholas. You see, she suffers from Bipolar Disorder. There have been times when she has refused to take her medication. That is what happened when she had disappeared in the past. But, the big difference between those other times and this time, is that she was never gone for more than two weeks before. She has been missing for months now. She has never done that! I don't think she would worry me like that. She's a good girl. She really is. Amber is troubled but she certainly is kind down to her soul!"

Cosette was hastily typing the wealth of information she was collecting into her trusty, new laptop.

"How would you describe your daughter's marriage?"

"My, they are so in love. Amber is crazy about her husband. My girl has always been very flirtatious. She lives for attention but her flirtations would never make her leave Nicholas. My daughter and I had coffee together about ten days before her disappearance. She told me how much she loves being married. They were about to try to start a family. I know my daughter. Her eyes can't lie to me. I see every emotion in them. There is no tricking a mom. She meant every word she said. She is happy. I am telling you, Cosette! Amber did not leave voluntarily and nobody can convince me otherwise."

Cosette collected the names and contact information for Amber's friends, associates and coworkers. Feeling satisfied that she had covered all the critical questions, Cosette thanked the grieving lady for the valuable information she had provided and returned back to her office.

10

He returned to his home and made a bee-line to the terrarium located in the center of his dimly lit bedroom.

"Hey, buddy! How has your day been?"

He excitedly greeted his treasured Rosy Boa Snake, Roper.

Roper had been his pet for six years. He was his best friend and he made a point of spending time with the serpent at every opportunity he had. Roper loved to strangle and consume live mice and rats. He would make sure to always be present when his pet was feasting. He often cheered him on while screaming, "Rope her." Using a spin on the snake's name from Roper to "Rope her" during the pet's kills was meant to be a nod to the fact that they both relished strangling and consuming. They were a team. He loved Roper more than he currently loved anyone in his life.

Now, he was beginning to come down from the high of his slaying on the trail earlier that day. The aching weight of fatigue flooded his muscles and caused his eyelids to droop. He fell onto his lumpy mattress and curled into a tight ball. His final thoughts were of Patsy's horror filled face. The image made him chuckle softly and he drifted into a deep, peaceful slumber.

Cosette arrived at her second day of work bright and early. She was the first one in the office. Her goal was to get a jump start on the Amber Trident case. Raquel, Amber's mother, was living rent-free in her head ever since their meeting yesterday. As a mother herself, she couldn't even begin to fathom the pain the grieving lady must be experiencing.

Cosette could not legally hack into social media accounts. She could, however, observe all of the public activity such as posts and comments. She filled an oversized mug with coffee and then added a generous tablespoon of brown sugar to the liquid. This gave the drink a distinct caramel-like flavor which awoke her senses and was soothing all at the same time.

Let's get down to business. I have an afternoon chalked full of interviews with different people in Amber's life. I have no time to waste.

First, she visited Amber's Facebook page. She noted that she had 538 friends and that she had the tendency to generally post on a weekly basis. The day before she went missing she posted an inspirational quote.

"You can't go back and change the beginning, but you can start where you are and change the ending." C.S. Lewis

Hmm, that is an interesting quote considering she vanished into thin air the very next day. The quote hints at new beginnings. Could she possibly have left voluntarily?

Cosette still wasn't convinced that she did indeed leave by free will. *A mother's intuition is usually accurate and Raquel was certain that there was foul play involved with her daughter's disappearance. Plus, if she had left on her own, wouldn't there be some trace of activity such as charges on a credit card or bank account activity?*

One of the first things she had learned at the police academy was that it is very difficult for a person to go entirely off the grid. Cosette continued to analyze the social media pages of Amber's friends. There was one man in particular, Ryan Pinto, who engaged regularly on Amber's page. He often left the fire or heart eye emojis in the comment sections and he loved each and every one of her posts during the past several years. Cosette researched him further online and discovered that he was in his early thirties and lived in the Keys, a waterfront, gated community located in South Lake Tahoe. She knew it was a shot in the dark but she refused to leave a single stone unturned. She was determined to discover where Amber was. Her family deserved closure.

11

Tinsley was enjoying her morning coffee while snuggled under a blanket of soft Welsh wool. The steaming liquid warmed her belly. The rich scent of her roasted Arabic coffee beans always revitalized her. Tinsley gazed out the window and noticed that the tree branches rustled from a gentle breeze. It was a cloudless day and the sun appeared as a tangy, orange orb in the dawn sky. She scooped up the remote from the end table next to her and flipped on the television. Breaking news was flashing on every local station. Her interest became piqued. An image of a lady Tinsley estimated to be in her mid thirties filled the thirty-two inch flat screen.

Tinsley turned up the volume. The newscaster's perfectly coiffed, copper, red hair tumbled over her shoulders. Her bubbly expressions and upbeat presentation was a clear mismatch to the tragic story she was reporting about.

A young lady had been found deceased on a nearby trail in South Lake Tahoe. She had been strangled. Tinsley felt saddened and uneasy by the hiker's horrific demise. She recalled that not too long ago there had been a rash of killings in the nearby Virginia City area. The man had been arrested so, of course, he couldn't be responsible for this killing. Perhaps this murder was an isolated incident, Tinsley hoped. Maybe she had a vicious ex-husband. It was time for her to prepare for her shift at the casino. She vowed she would google this murder in more detail after work.

Tinsley's shift was slow and monotonous. She had some downtime to banter with Roseanne and Melissa. After the shift, she attended the annual party which the casino threw for its employees. The shindig was held in an opulent ballroom overlooking the spellbinding lake. Its ceiling dripped with high end Czech chandeliers. The party was an ideal chance for Tinsley to catch up with her coworkers. An added bonus was that Peter would be by her side.

Tinsley slipped into a figure hugging, turquoise evening gown. After giving herself an appreciative glance in the powder room mirror, she met up with Peter inside the Lakeshore Ballroom. He looked dapper in his suit. His entire face lit up when he spotted her. Tinsley knew that he was still in love with her. She often secretly wondered if ending her romantic relationship with him years ago had been a grave error. He treated her like a queen. They could talk about anything and everything and, she had to admit to herself, that their passion had been earth-shattering during the time period when they were lovers. She was a fool to have broken up with him and she knew it. Tinsley had been seeing a therapist on a regular basis. She had discovered through her sessions that due to some major childhood trauma, deep down, she did not feel she deserved to be in a healthy, loving relationship. Tinsley was more likely to embark on a relationship with a man who did not treat her with respect. She had always been drawn to the bad boys.

Enough of your over-analysis! She scolded herself*. What's done is done. Now go and have a fun night.*

She slid her arm coyly through Peter's and he proudly escorted her over to the bartending station. Then, they sat at a corner booth.

Peter's face visibly dropped and his brow furrowed as Gabe, the pool attendant, slinked over to them. God, he hated that man. Without asking, Gabe scooted into the booth next to Tinsley. He sat way too close to her for Peter's liking. Tinsley lit up like an airport runway.

"Well, hello handsome. Fancy seeing you here!" Her statement caused her to erupt into flirtatious giggles. Peter had to make an effort not to roll his eyes at her obvious display of affection.

"I was hoping you'd be here, beauty. Your glass is looking a little low. May I get you a refill?"

Gabe's statement started an evening of suggestive banter between the duo. Peter felt like a 5th wheel. They went out on the dance floor during George Michael's, "Careless Whisper" song. Tinsley was clinging to Gabe as if he was a flotation device and she had just survived a jetliner crash in the middle of the Atlantic Ocean.

*Why don't you just get a room?*Peter thought bitterly.

The temptation to storm out rose within him but then he remembered that tragic news report which was splashed on the front page of every local newspaper.

A killer was on the loose and Peter was not about to let the love of his life go home unescorted. However, at the rate Gabe and Tinsley were going, she may very well have company tonight, he thought glumly.

Moments later, Tyler, the parking attendant, entered the room and darted straight for Tinsley.

Tinsley *really is in her element when she is the center of attention. Could this night get any worse?* Peter splashed back another shot of straight vodka.

12

The next few weeks passed by in a blur for Cosette. She was putting in at least fourteen hours a day at work. So far, she had not uncovered anything ground breaking about Amber or her disappearance. She was starting to see why law enforcement had chalked her case up to a voluntary departure. Yet, something within her just couldn't give up, not yet, anyway. She had interviewed Ryan Pinto, among many of the other missing woman's acquaintances. Ryan had been friends with Amber since childhood. After Cosette spent many hours analyzing their relationship, she was convinced that their union was strictly platonic. In addition, Ryan had been visiting Scotland during the time of Amber's disappearance. He had an airtight alibi.

Through Cosette's extensive research, she had gathered that, although Amber had several male friends and she had remained mildly flirtatious despite her nuptials to Nicholas, she had not engaged in an affair or partaken in anything which would be considered high risk behavior. Amber's disappearance made her head spin. Sadly, Tommy had not uncovered anything of interest in his research either. They looked at each other from across their desks and both could feel the weight of their heavy workloads. Tommy's bloodshot eyes burned from a deep fatigue. He rubbed his temples and sighed. Cosette guzzled coffee throughout the day in order to keep up her energy. The endless flow of caffeine allowed her to continue to give 100% to their first case.

Cosette's eyes fell on the dog calendar behind Tommy. Since they were taking a few minutes to relax, she finally asked her dear friend,

"Tommy, I have noticed your 2010 calendar from day one. Why are there exclamation marks all over the box for the 23rd of May?"

"Have I never told you about my Rhodesian Ridgebacks? My beloved dog, Skye, gave birth to the eight most beautiful puppies I have ever seen on May 23rd in 2010. It was a very special day for me. In fact, it was such a great experience that I decided to do it all over again. My new dog, Mabel, is due to have her litter in just two weeks from now," Tommy beamed.

Cosette carefully studied the featured Ridgeback for the month of May.

"They really are an exquisite breed. Are they loyal? Are they good with children?"

"Heck, yeah! They are the best breed!" insisted Tommy.

Cosette had always longed for her own dog. Spencer had been asking for a puppy since he first learned how to speak. Cosette hesitated but felt overwhelmed by the desire to have one of Tommy's puppies.

"Are the puppies all claimed for already?" Cosette asked with nervous anticipation.

"We are expecting Mabel to deliver eight puppies. I have seven families who have already submitted their deposits. That means, I still have one puppy remaining."

Tommy winked slyly. He was such a good man and she enjoyed working with him a great deal. He always had Cosette's best interest at heart.

"Let me bounce it off of Luke tonight. Since we are getting married soon, it will be his pup also. I do have to say, that I would be honored to be able to adopt one of your puppies. May I give you an update on Luke's response tomorrow?"

"I'll tell you what, I will keep the eighth puppy safe and sound and reserved for you. Whenever you know the verdict, just let me know."

13

The South Lake Tahoe Police Department was a flurry of activity.

Tommy's uncle, Sutter Munro, called an emergency meeting with a handful of his officers and detectives.

They filed into the station's largest conference room.

Looking stern, Mr. Munro commenced the meeting.

"As I'm sure most of you have heard by now, we had a brutal slaying of a young lady by the name of Patsy Goodwin."

He turned on the overhead projector and presented the victim's photo.

"She was discovered this morning by a hiker on the Glen Alpine Trail. Her husband, Jeff Goodwin, reported her missing last night. He discovered she was not at home when he returned from work at approximately 6:30 p.m. He suspected that she had gone on a hike but he was not sure which trail she had actually hiked on or whether she had even made it to the intended destination. What I'm about to disclose to all of you cannot get out to the media under any circumstances. I want this information kept close to the vest. Only the killer will know the following details of the crime scene. By keeping it quiet, we can weed out false confessions as well. We all know that there are always those looney tunes that will claim they are the killer when in fact they are not."

The room did a collective nod in agreement with Sutter's statement.

"Mrs. Goodwin's body was found posed along the creek off of the main path at about the 1.2 mile mark. Her arms and hands were folded onto her chest in a praying position. In addition, a silver necklace with a pendant of the zodiac sign, Aquarius, was placed on the bottom of her neck."

The chief displayed an image of the necklace.

The third image depicted the crime scene.

"Note the ligature marks on the victim's neck. This was overkill. The item used to strangle her had such extreme pressure applied to it that it embedded almost one inch into her flesh. Now, here is the doozy, the most concerning part. Officer McConlin ran all this information through the national database earlier today. Caprice Lansing, a twenty-eight year old woman was discovered four months ago on a trail in the Henderson, Nevada area. The crime scene was nearly identical to Patsy Goodwin's. Lansing was strangled and a silver Aquarius pendant was discovered on her throat. Their local police department has dubbed this killer, "The Water Bearer". That's the symbol of the Aquarius zodiac sign. Since the signatures at both scenes were virtually identical we can be almost certain that the same killer took the lives of both of these young ladies. The medical examiner inspected Mrs. Goodwin's corpse as soon as she was brought in this morning. I will have a lot more information once he reports his findings back to me. Let's meet here again tomorrow afternoon at 4:00. In the interim, I would like Officer Sleet to poke around in Patsy's husband's background. I want to find out every last detail about him. Also, Sleet, find out where he was, at all times, yesterday."

Officer Sleet gave a thumbs up to assure the chief that he understood his assignment.

14

Dr. Westford had been the medical examiner in the area for thirty-six years. He was highly respected in his field and often had to testify in local murder cases. Despite his extensive experience, it still saddened him to see a life viciously cut short by a ruthless killer. He surveyed the young lady laying lifeless on the metal table. Out of respect, he always covered the parts of the body he wasn't currently examining. They deserved dignity in death as well. He treated them the way he would want his own loved ones to be treated. A striking feature of this murder was how deep the ligature marks descended into the victim's throat. He collected fibers from the area in hopes of determining what sort of strangulation apparatus was used. Dr. Westford continued his examination of the corpse. He collected countless samples for further testing. The kind hearted physician was briefed that Mrs. Goodwin was discovered by a hiker at 8:00a.m. The examination indicated that not only was the corpse in a state of full rigor mortis but her core was already cold. Under normal conditions, it takes approximately fifteen hours for a body to go into the rigor mortis stage. However, for a corpse to cool all the way to the core it takes roughly twenty-four hours. Armed with this information, the doctor was certain that the victim had died during the morning hours of the previous day. One reason this information was crucial was because it allowed law enforcement to focus in on the alibis of people of interest within a certain time frame. Dr. Westward had discovered one of the key puzzle pieces.

The heartbroken man sat in his darkened bedroom on the grungy floor and stared at the faded photo with a flashlight.

She was so beautiful. I still love her. Why did she have to betray me like that? I would have spent every day for the rest of our lives making her happier than she even knew was possible.

He felt an intense, searing pain in his heart. She had destroyed him. All that was left of him was a cracked shell. Memories flooded back. His grief had a tendency to haunt him on a daily basis.

The groom was waiting at the Saint Matthew's Church altar, looking more striking than ever in his high end tuxedo and thick, perfectly styled hair. His entire body shook due to his intense happiness and anticipation. The day had finally arrived. In just a few more minutes, the love of his life would saunter down the aisle. They would declare their eternal love for each other and then she would be his bride forever.

But, that never happened. She left me at the altar, ran off with some punk and destroyed me. I was left humiliated and heartbroken.

Friends and family had even flown in from all over the country to attend our nuptials. My life ended that day.

He blotted at his hot, bitter tears with a threadbare, permanently stained handkerchief. Then, he swigged back a shot of Tahoe Blue Vodka and drank himself into a state of delirium once again.

Nicholas Trident needed an evening out. He was perpetually depressed and riddled with high levels of anxiety. All he ever thought about was his missing wife. He was fixated on Amber and her whereabouts for the majority of every day and night. At this point in his life, he considered three hours of shut-eye an acceptable amount of sleep. He jumped into the steaming hot shower, shaved and put on jeans, a white t-shirt and a black leather jacket. This was the first time he had spruced up his appearance since Amber went missing. He got in his car and zipped to the Crystal Waters Casino. Nicholas positioned himself at one of the slot machines and mindlessly pulled the crank on his machine. A cocktail waitress meandered over to him within a few minutes.

"What can I get you, good lookin'?"

Nicholas peered up and was taken aback by the server's appearance. His eyes devoured her beauty. Her name tag had "Tinsley" printed in silver, block letters.

"Well, hello there, Tinsley. Could you get me a scotch on the rocks and keep 'em coming?"

"You bet," she winked seductively.

Tinsley went back to the server station and whispered excitedly to Roseanne,

"You have got to check out the Greek god I am serving over by the slot machines. He looks just like a movie star."

Roseanne took a spin around the pit and knew instantly who Tinsley was referring to. Men that looked like that were a rarity.

"Tinsley, you were not exaggerating! My goodness gracious!"

The ladies giggled and then Tinsley delivered the first cocktail to Nicholas. The last hour of her shift was grueling. The area became inundated with guests after a convention meeting had ended at the nearby conference room. They all wanted their drinks and they expected quick service. Tinsley let out a sigh of relief when her shift finally came to a close. She hadn't forgotten about the handsome mystery man and after freshening up her makeup she took the quickest route over to where he was sitting. They had some relaxed, flirtatious banter. His yearning for her was apparent. Nicholas reminded Tinsley of a wolf who was dying of starvation. Their chemistry was palpable.

The couple raced to his home. Nicholas was losing all self control as he handed Tinsley the keys to his front door. They both felt dizzy and feverish with anticipation. They landed clumsily onto the sofa in the living room. Tinsley grunted in discomfort as she bumped her tailbone on the arm of the leather furniture piece but she forced herself to brush the pain aside. Their passion was intense but short lived. During the night, they headed up to the master bedroom. Nicholas fell asleep instantly. Tinsley lay there, sprawled out and completely motionless. A wave of remorse and self pity pulled at her heart.

What is wrong with me? Sure, Nicholas is a good looking man but this evening together could not have been more meaningless. I'm a fool. I know that I am in love with Peter but I am doing everything I can to destroy any chance of ever being with him. I'm pretty sure my life is the definition of having hit rock bottom. I cant go on living like this. Something has to change.

Tears welled within her painfully fatigued eyes. The droplets flowed down her face, streaking the heavy coat of foundation caked on her skin and trickled onto the fleece sheets.

15

The next day, Tinsley moped through her shift. On most days, she forced herself to be ultra charming to the clients but today she could not muster up the enthusiasm. Peter did his usual rounds throughout the shift and visited with Tinsley. He knew that something was off with her mood. Concern furrowed his features. She was not about to confess to him that she had indulged in a casual encounter the previous evening and she definitely was not going to admit her feelings of love for her lifelong friend.

Tinsley fibbed and told Peter that she currently had a vicious headache and that this was the cause of her less than jovial mood.

Roseanne had been updated on every detail of her friend's night and she was briefed to not mention the encounter to Peter. She had been a loyal friend to Tinsley for years. She always had her back and was there for her unwaveringly.

Roseanne's shift was finally over. She bid her somber friend goodbye and then she headed home to her lakefront cottage. It was a sunny and peaceful day. The sky was cloudless and turquoise in color. In just a few minutes, she arrived at her cherished property. It was nestled in the woods and overlooked the shimmering lake. Roseanne walked a short, curved trail to the front door. The trees above entwined with each other as if they were dancing together. She always felt like she was walking through a mystical forest. Roseanne entered her residence and let out a sigh of relief. Her home was her sanctuary. The cottage was spotless, gleaming actually. It was light and bright and the fresh breeze from the pine trees floated into the home.

Roseanne strived to live a "Marie Kondo" type of lifestyle. Her home was peaceful and free of clutter. She spent much of her free-time organizing and decluttering her closets and drawers. Filtered light glinted through the large, oval shaped, crystal clean windows. The fatigue from the day was beginning to take its toll on her. Roseanne plodded to the master bedroom and eased back onto her satin, overstuffed pillows. Her muscles ached and she stretched like a content kitten. She unintentionally drifted into a light sleep. The next time she opened her eyes she was immersed in darkness. She startled and was disappointed that she had allowed sleep to take over.

This won't do. Now that I napped, it will be almost impossible for me to fall asleep tonight and I have an early shift tomorrow morning. The only chance I have of getting some decent shut-eye later is if I exercise now and tire myself out.

With that thought, Roseanne lifted herself off of the bed, pulled on her exercise clothes and exited through the front door. The sun had already bid its nightly farewell to the quaint, lake town. The glowing lights from some of the neighbors' homes and an occasional street lantern, illuminated her way. She walked down to the lake. The water was autumn silver in color and its surface was statue still. The occasional sound of trouts dive bombing in the distance broke the silence. The ground thistle prickled Roseanne's calves. Hungry mosquitoes swirled around her head. The sweet smell of tree sap mixed with wild grown mint mingled in the air. It was an alpine lake. The snow tipped mountain peaks cradled their arms of rock beneath the lake and supported it the way a mother cuddles her newborn child. The serene, idyllic setting was a sharp contrast from the thunderously loud, smoky environment of the casino. Roseanne was so engrossed in pleasant thoughts that she didn't detect the slow but steady approach of the looming, cloaked figured. A strong, broad hand clasped her shoulder urgently. She spun around to face the menacing opponent. Illumination from a nearby cabin afforded Roseanne a glimpse of the monster's features. An evil sneer split his face. His sharklike eyes were hallows of madness, full of loathing and evil.

Roseanne's eyes bulged with fright. Before she was able to exhale a shriek of terror, her entire world went dark.

16

Adam Zhao arrived at his place of business just as the sun was beginning to make its daily ascent into the crystal sky. He had owned, "Up and Adam Jet Ski Rentals" for over a decade already. It was a thriving business and a favorite among locals. Adam entered his one room office and checked his voicemails and emails. Then he went out to inspect his collection of fourteen jet skis. Part of his inspections included ensuring that his fleet had not been damaged over the nighttime. Sadly, local teenagers had been vandalizing his property recently. He also checked the throttle cables of each jet ski to verify that they were in working order before his first clients of the morning arrived. He trekked down to the dock. In the distance, Adam spotted an unidentifiable mass splayed out near the shoreline. He was startled by the unusual sight and darted over to it. As he approached the mystery figure, terror sealed his throat. A young woman was sprawled near the water's edge. The waves rippled at her gleaming white tennis shoes. Her mouth gaped open. Adam shivered. He knew that she was deceased and he dialed 911. He stuttered his words to the operator and had a difficult time breathing due to the panic which was hijacking his body.

Later that afternoon, Cosette was engrossed in her work when Frank burst into the office.

"Cosette, Tommy, something big has happened. Another young lady was found deceased on the shores of Lake Tahoe this morning. The medical examiner has determined that the same killer brutally murdered both ladies and law enforcement is convinced that we are dealing with a serial killer. A tell-tale Aquarius zodiac sign necklace was left on the corpse of both of the victims. I would like for you to head over to the South Lake Tahoe Police Department. They need all hands on deck. They are having a meeting in exactly one hour. That should give you enough time to get there."

Tommy's uncle was the chief of the South Lake Tahoe Police Department. It was not unusual for him to enlist Frank's assistance with higher profile cases over the years.

Cosette and Tommy drove to the police department. Due to some stop and go traffic along their route, they arrived with only a few minutes to spare. The duo found their way to the conference room.

They had attended a few law enforcement meetings during police academy. It normally consisted of coffee, snacks and painted on smiles. This meeting felt different to Cosette. There was a distinct electricity in the air. The energy and anxiety in the room was palpable. The low-ceilinged, stark white chamber was filled beyond capacity with people from various positions in law enforcement. The sun faded, cobalt blue drapes swayed hypnotically from the gentle mid-summer breeze. The scent of deodorant and after shave, filled the space. Cosette and Tommy were able to take a seat in the last two vacant chairs. Sutter Munro commenced the meeting,

"First, I would like to thank you all for getting here with such short notice. We have a lot of ground to cover. For those of you who aren't aware, another victim, Roseanne Buchanan, was discovered on a local beach early this morning. The perp strangled her with a rope. An Aquarius zodiac sign pendant and chain were put on her corpse. The victim was placed adjacent to a body of water, just as Patsy Goodwin was. Her corpse was left staged as well. Her arms were placed on her chest in a praying position. As I mentioned at our last meeting, through various data searches, we have been able to ascertain that one other victim from Henderson, Nevada, was also discovered in the identical state as our local victims were. The similarities include the zodiac necklace, method of death was strangulation and her body was also left by a pond on a trail in that area. We have now officially ruled these cases as serial killer related. I would like to introduce Dr. Ann Jackson, a world renowned forensic psychologist. She would like to brief all of us on some key insights about these cases. An elegant, ebony haired lady with flawless mocha skin and dazzling fawn like eyes, confidently approached the podium.

"Good afternoon, I know we all have a lot of work ahead of us, so, I will not keep you too long. After reviewing the case files for the three murders which Captain Munro just discussed, I am convinced, beyond a shadow of a doubt, that we are dealing with a serial killer. The facts of these cases have never been released to the public. Therefore, it would be impossible for a copy cat murderer to be involved with the subsequent killings. The signature at each murder scene is virtually identical. That is not a coincidence. As experienced law enforcement officials, I know you all are aware that there are four types of serial killers.

Hedonistic
Mission-oriented
Visionary

and Power-control seekers

"Based on my research, I am certain that we are dealing with an organized, hedonistic serial killer. What that means, is that the killer is an individual who murders for the thrill and pleasure of the act. These type of killers will typically use weapons which allow them close contact with their victims. Strangulation is a very common method for the hedonistic killer. This is, of course, the method the killer in our case utilized. Often these types will fantasize for years about homicide before they actually perform the act. Their desire to murder dominates their thoughts. Once, they kill, they will be driven to kill again. Also, the time space between the slayings will progressively shorten. In other words, we are in a time crunch. The killer will act again and if I had to guess, it will happen quite soon."

Dr. Jackson continued, "Our victims all had deep wounds in their necks from strangulation and the fact that over 90% of serial killers are men, I am betting that our perp is a male. This was overkill and a great deal of strength and fury was utilized. Also, he more than likely has an above average I.Q. Yet, he probably did poorly academically and has a difficult time holding down a steady job as an adult. There is a high chance that he is employed as an unskilled worker or he might even be unemployed. We should focus on any individual who has a record of starting fires, has a history of voyeurism or torturing animals."

Cosette inputted all of the details into her laptop. She had never fathomed that she would be involved in a serial killing case this early in her career. Due to her best friend's demise, her primary passion related to her job was to bring these monsters to justice. The desire to catch this killer rose within her.

Captain Munro came back to the podium and thanked the brilliant psychologist for her thorough briefing.

He continued, "Dr Westford, the medical examiner, has given me a preliminary report about Ms. Buchanan's homicide. As you are all aware, several of the tests will take weeks, if not months, to process. However, the doctor was already able to provide us with invaluable information. The ropes used to strangle all three of the victims consisted of a nylon material. The width of the rope, in each case, was 9/16th of an inch. The killer exerted a great deal of strength with his hands and forearms which impaired the exchange of gases and ultimately caused asphyxia. Our killer caused complete compression of the trachea in all three of the cases. Ms. Goodwin had significant bruising of her thumbs, indicating that she fought for her life. During the struggle, she scooped her thumbs under the rope in hopes of preventing the strangulation. Ms. Buchanan and Ms. Lansing, the victim from Henderson, Nevada, did not have thumb bruising or any other obvious signs that they had struggled. Most likely, they were attacked before they even knew what hit them. He struck quickly and without warning with both of the ladies. Mrs. Goodwin must have had some sort of warning that he was approaching. Either he spoke to her first or she spotted a suspicious person in the vicinity. I am going to need all hands on deck. It is critical that we act on this case quickly before more innocent people get killed. I would like some of you to regularly monitor the trail systems and beaches. We need to interview any and all associates of the three murder victims. That includes family, friends, coworkers, neighbors and exes. Let's see if we can find a common thread between the victims."

17

It was Tinsley's day off and she had spent most of the day catching up on much needed sleep. She finally opened her eyes and felt as groggy as a groundhog coming slowly out of hibernation. She reached for her phone and squinted at the clock. It was time to get up. She was meeting Peter at the restaurant in just an hour from now. She traipsed to the bathroom and turned on the shower. As soon as the room was enveloped in steam, she entered the shower enclosure and positioned herself under the stream. The searing water pelted her skin. Once her hair was fully drenched, she massaged her favorite pomegranate scented shampoo onto her scalp. The purple color of the product was always off putting for her but she knew it was great for preventing brassiness in her bleached blond hair. Her shower experience was topped off with a deep conditioning mask and a raspberry scented body wash. She wrapped her locks into a towel and headed for the well stocked makeup table. After applying a thick coat of makeup onto her skin and eyes, she blow dried her hair. For the final touch, she used a curling iron to create beach waves. Tinsley scrunched her hair and added a final spritz of hair spray. She was impressed with how perfect her hair looked. It had the ideal messy beach look, a perfect vibe for the current warm weather and festive mood she was in. The doorbell chimed and startled her. Still naked as a jay bird, she slipped into her Egyptian cotton robe. Tinsley was not expecting any visitors. She tiptoed to the front door and peered out of the peephole. To her surprise, Peter was standing there. She eagerly swung the door open. What Tinsley saw, stunned her. Peter's skin looked pale and pasty. His eyes were puffy and damp.

"Peter? What is wrong?"

"Can I come in?"

"Of course, you can. You have me a little worried. What is going on?"

She motioned for him to sit on the nearest sofa. Peter was visibly shaken. His forehead was coated with perspiration. He slumped onto the seat and placed his face into the palm of his hands. Tinley's feeling of alarm was building more with each passing second.

"I just got a call from my manager at the casino. Something horrible has happened. Rose...Anne...is dead."

Tinsley whimpered and screamed out,

"What? What on earth happened?"

"She was murdered, found on the beach near her home this morning. I can't believe this happened. She had her entire life in front of her still."

Time seemed to stop. Tinsley felt a radiating pain in her chest. She teetered onto Peter's shoulder and exploded into a deluge of tears. He pulled her close to him and clung to her as if he would never let her go. They wept for what felt like hours, lost in each other's agony and grief.

Cosette made Luke's favorite supper, Shepherd's Pie. Spencer was at a friend's house, so, this was the ideal time to talk to him about possibly adopting one of Tommy's puppies. Luke was in a great mood but that was hardly unusual. Her fiancé was one of the most perpetually optimistic people she had ever known. If a happiness gene did, in fact, exist, then, he definitely was one of the lucky people to possess it. They sat outside at the dining table by the infinity pool. After some discussion about the day's events, Cosette asked Luke if he had ever heard of the Rhodesian Ridgeback dog breed.

"Of course, that is a great breed. They are originally from Zimbabwe. What makes you ask about them?"

"Well, Tommy's Ridgeback is about to have a litter and he said we could have one of the puppies, if we were interested."

Cosette held her breath in eager anticipation of Luke's response."I know that Spencer is praying to have a dog too," she continued.

Luke's eyes illuminated with excitement.

"That is a great idea. I would love for us to add a pup to our family. Tell Tommy we are all in. We can surprise Spencer!"

Cosette was ecstatic. She could not wait to tell Tommy that they would, in fact, be able to adopt one of his puppies. The couple spent the remainder of their evening researching Rhodesian Ridgebacks and reading tips on how to care for and train a new puppy. They could not wait to surprise Spencer with the good news when he got home.

Cosette was working long hours every day. The newly minted detective was determined not to leave a stone unturned in the serial killer case. She divided her work hours between the homicides and finding Amber Trident's location. Her days were an interesting mix of desk work and interviews. With Frank's guidance, Tommy and Cosette became more fine-tuned at investigative procedures. They were the ideal team. When one of them became stumped about something, the other one was there to support and brainstorm with the other. When both were at a dead end, Tommy would pull out a bowl of Flaming Hot Cheetos, the dart board, a Winmau Blade 5, and his shiny, green darts with the letter "T" inscribed on each feather. He spent several years in England and loved everything about the beautiful country. He spoke of his time there often. He had developed a passion for darts or "oche" as they were often referred to by the British. When Cosette and Tommy played the game together, their minds cleared and they had a tendency to reset. After their good natured competitions, they had more energy again and were able to move full steam ahead.

After a working lunch together, Cosette bid Tommy farewell and headed to her first interview of the day. She was traveling to Incline Village, a picturesque town located on the eastern north shore of Lake Tahoe to interview Patsy Goodwin's sister, Eliza Whedon. The town was situated on an enclave and the residents were known for their relaxed and genteel lifestyle. Cosette parallel parked along the curb in front of the stunning mountain retreat. Views of the lake filtered through the pine tress in the front yard. She rang on the door and within seconds a stylish and refined looking platinum blonde answered. Her hair was pulled up into a high ponytail. Curtain bangs framed her lovely face. She had haunting, steel-blue eyes, thick, jet black lashes and perfect porcelain skin complete with invisible pores and a silk-like skin tone. Her voice quivered as she said,

"Good afternoon, I'm Eliza Whedon. You must be Cosette DuPont?"

The ladies shook hands and Cosette was escorted into the living room of the impressive home. The entire back wall consisted of a crystal clear sheet of glass which afforded million dollar views of iconic Lake Tahoe. To the left, stood a wall mounted aquarium about the size of Cosette's closet. Seahorses, Coral Blennies and Puffer Fish were the colorful residents of the enclosure. The detective was in awe of the striking display.

The kitchen island was full of flowers and plants of various kinds offered as condolence gifts for Patsy's death. The grieving sister lowered herself onto the rich, mahogany, leather seat. It was evident that she was mustering up all her strength not to burst into tears.

After expressing her heartfelt sympathy, Cosette began to interview Eliza. They spoke about Patsy's past, her recent friendships and the state of her marriage to Jeff.

"Patsy and Jeff adored each other. She fell in love with him on their first date and that was not like my sister. She had been in other relationships before him, and still had not fallen in love with those men, even after six months or a year. Jeff swept Patsy off of her feet. My sister always had everything going for her. She was popular in school and achieved straight A's easily. She got into her top choice college and met the man of her dreams. Patsy was almost constantly in a good mood."

"The first real obstacle she had to face was infertility. My sister had always longed to have several children one day. Her heart broke when after years of trying for a baby, it still did not happen. That was the only time in Patsy's life when she had to deal with any significant anxiety and sadness."

"How did infertility effect her marriage?"

"Well, sure they were stressed sometimes. It definitely took some of the romance out of their relationship but, all in all, they were still very much in love. They were each other's best friends and rarely quarreled."

"May I ask how you would describe your relationship with your sister?"

Tears welled up in Eliza's almond shaped eyes. Her hand gripped the arm of the chair to the point that her skin whitened. It was clear to Cosette that Eliza was destroyed by her sister's passing.

"She was my closest friend. Patsy and I told each other everything and we always supported each other. One school year we even volunteered as Candy Stripers at a local hospital together. In our teens and early twenties, we often spent our summers in Bar Harbor, Maine, spending our days on the beach and our evenings on the decks of the various oceanfront restaurants. We sure loved the stuffed, baked lobster with garlic butter. Going to Chinese restaurants was another one of our favorite activities. The great memories we shared together are countless."

Tears baptized Eliza's face. Cosette gave a comforting squeeze to her slumped shoulder.

The hardest part of her new career was seeing the pain of the family members of murder victims. Cosette completed the interview shortly thereafter and headed back to her vehicle.

The drive back to the office was an opportune time to ponder and analyze all of the information she had received from Eliza. Patsy did not have any clear enemies. Everyone around her seemed to genuinely like her including college friends and ex-boyfriends. Her husband, Jeff, based on extensive interviews and computer research, was clearly faithful to her throughout their entire marriage. Patsy appeared to have been faithful as well. With that in mind, one could eliminate a jealous mistress or lover, at this point.

18

Tommy was eagerly awaiting Cosette's return. She entered the office and was greeted by him. He was brimming over with excitement.

Tommy exclaimed, "I have been waiting for you on pins and needles. Please have a seat. You need to hear this."

Cosette's interest was piqued.

"Ok, after you left, I went to interview Roseanne Buchanan's brother, James Buchanan. Boy, did he have an earful to tell me. His sister was dating this creep, August Winters, for about a year. They broke up recently and apparently he has been full on stalking her. He even left a dead rat in her mailbox. He would show up everywhere she went and send her threatening texts."

Cosette gasped, "Oh my gosh! Really?"

Tommy beamed with pride and stated,

"Fasten your seatbelt. You haven't heard the most interesting part yet. When I got back to the office, I right away started tinkering around on my computer. When I punched the dude's name into the internet, it lit up like fireworks. Catch this, August Winters follows none other than Caprice Lansing on Instagram. That is one hell of a coincidence. She lived near Vegas. That is pretty far from Lake Tahoe. Why would he know a random woman from the other side of the state? I mean, what are the odds? He is connected to at least two of our three victims. I am going to keep digging around and see if I can find a link between August and Patsy Goodwin. Then we'd have three for three."

Tommy was short of breath from his intense excitement. He took a long swig of his iced coffee drink and dabbed his forehead with a crumpled Taco Bell napkin. His enthusiasm was infectious. Cosette had to admit that what Tommy had uncovered could end up being the link they needed to identify and ultimately apprehend the killer.

August woke up at the crack of dawn with a monster of a headache. He was hungover again.

Well, the best way to cure a hangover is to get drunk all over again.

He laughed uproariously and headed to his liquor cabinet. Just seeing the rich, amber liquid calmed his frayed nerves. He poured the smooth, delicious potion into the largest glass he could find. He added two ice cubes and slouched back onto his bed. He read the article about his ex, Roseanne's, homicide for at least the 30th time. The words in the column hypnotized him. He was enchanted by the few details law enforcement had released.

Cops are always so darn stingy with the gory details of a murder. Roseanne got what she deserved. She had been playing me for a fool way too long. Ha! Karma can be awful!

His mind drifted back to childhood. He had an identical twin brother, Alex. Alex was scared of everything and August was fearless. They were as opposite as two boys could possibly be. He remembered the summer their parents took them to Lake Almanor in California. They had rented a small, but quaint cabin, directly on the lake. At night, August would drag his brother all over the adjacent woods. One evening, he spotted a fully grown Douglas Fir Tree near a clearing on the edge of the forest. A heavily used and aged tree house was teetering far up on the branches. August threw a fit so monumental with the objective to get Alex to accompany him up to the fort, that it made World War II look meek in comparison. Finally, Alex agreed and the twins climbed up to the desired spot. Alex's brow was dripping with sweat and his eyes were brimming with terror. After the boys sat precariously on the wobbly structure and August felt certain that his brother was starting to calm down, August jolted the board his twin was seated on and said,

"Bet you can't hold on!"

Alex slipped and tumbled down several feet before another branch cradled him. The young boy screamed with an intensity so extreme that it made nearby birds flutter up into the sky and the squirrels run for shelter. August felt pleased with himself for causing Alex's accident and snorted and hee-hawed until he felt as if his sides were about to split open.

His brother needed to go to the emergency room and the X-rays indicated that he had several fractured ribs.

August's father whipped him senseless that night. August had received beatings on a regular basis throughout his childhood.

A lot of good his discipline did. I am nastier and crueler than I've ever been. Alex deserved what he got. He was such a little do-gooder. Always trying to impress our parents. I showed him who the boss was. I was definitely the alpha male in the family and Alex knew it!

The thought satisfied him. August stumbled back to the cabinet and poured himself a generous refill. By noon, he was passed out on top of his unmade, grimy sheets.

19

Lightning flashed over the alpine town and sliced through the mountain tops. The air was filled with electricity. Thunder clapped and groaned as if it were discontent or suffering from some sort of physical ailment. The surface of the lake was covered intermittently with an intense yellow light from the lightning. It reminded Tinsley of lemon frosting smeared generously across a birthday cake. Rain pattered against her windows. The wind moaned and launched leaves and small branches through the air. It also caused the tall grass in the nearby meadow to roll similar to a wave when a speedboat passed by the docks. She continued to gaze outdoors. Her heart felt heavy and her head was congested, probably because she was starting to get a cold and also because crying had become her number one past-time since she had learned of Roseanne's murder.

Tinsley still couldn't believe that her dear friend was gone, forever. One moment, they were laughing and gossiping together during their shift. The next, she was found deceased on a beach. As much as she needed the money, she had requested some time off from the casino. Her grief was overwhelming. She did not have it in her to doll herself up and act syrupy sweet with customers all day. Tinsley figured she would find a way to pay her bills for the month. She was like a cat. She always landed on her feet and managed somehow.

Immediately after breakfast the next morning, Cosette and Tommy made their way to August Winters' house. His home was a small, remote cabin located in the center of a thicket. The closest neighbors were at least a quarter of a mile away. Cosette shivered as they approached the abode. The structure reminded her of something in a horror movie. She whispered to Tommy,

"You could scream "bloody murder" out here for hours and nobody would ever hear you."

Tommy nodded in agreement.

Light was unable to filter into the canopy due to the heavy foliage. The front windows of the home were small, dark and filled with shadows which played tricks on their eyes. The tall pines stretched up like pointy knives into the sky. The area had its share of dead trees and plants as well. Branches creaked and leaves rustled as the detectives took the path to their destination. They could hear animals rooting in the underbrush.

A squirrel raced past the duo. A pond sat adjacent to the cabin. It was full of algae and mosquito larvae. Clearly, it had not been tended to in quite some time.

The cabin was made entirely of logs. The front door was covered with cobwebs and thick dust which had accumulated for months, if not years.

Tommy knocked and stepped back from the entrance. There was no response. He knocked again but this time more insistently. The door creaked open and a daunting, large man peered out. He was bald and had unkempt facial hair. His eyes were cold and bloodshot. His mouth was turned down into a scowl. As he hissed at them, "What do you want?" Cosette detected the strong odor of liquor coming off of his breath.

After brief introductions and an explanation as to why they were there, Cosette was pleasantly surprised to see that August allowed them into his home. He motioned for them to sit at the wobbly, small kitchen table as he moved two empty Jack Daniels bottles off of the table's surface. The air was stale and thick with cigarette smoke. A television blared in the background. The detectives could hear a fist fight in progress on the Jerry Springer show at a deafening volume.

"So, what do you two want?" barked the brutish man.

Cosette explained to him that they were involved in an active investigation of the recent rash of homicides in the area.

She stated, "Were you in a romantic relationship with one of the victims, Roseanne Buch-?" Before she could completely finish her statement, August roared with laughter and said, "Is that what this is all about? You're here because someone did this world a favor and got rid of that miserable woman?"

The detectives were taken aback by the man's callous attitude.

Tommy inquired, "Why would you say that the world is better off without Roseanne Buchanan?"

"She was a waste of space. We were together for a while. Those were months out of my life that I will never get back again. She dumped me, said I wasn't attentive enough to her. Ungrateful woman! Not to mention, Roseanne was such a black widow, that I'm surprised she didn't kill me after we mated."

Cosette, mortified about August's black widow comment, tried to get the man to refocus.

"There are reports which indicate that you harassed her a great deal up until the time of her death."

"Harassed is a term used loosely nowadays. In the past, it was seen as chivalrous to pursue a woman. Now you're looked at as some kind of creep."

"You think it's chivalrous to leave a rat in a woman's mailbox?" chimed Tommy.

August roared his signature laugh. "What? Ya got to keep a woman on her toes. I figured she might think I'm the man of her dreams after all when she compared me to a stinking, rotting rodent. It didn't work out that way, but it was worth a shot. Maybe next time, I'll give a woman a mushy Hallmark Card, long stemmed roses and French Champagne instead."

Cosette continued, "Where were you on June 7th between the hours of four in the afternoon and midnight?"

"I was here, at home. I'm always here."

Tommy continued, "Can anyone verify that you were indeed here?"

"Only the coyotes and the opossums." August chuckled again.

Cosette felt frustrated. It was clear the detectives were simply going around in circles with their line of questioning. She had one last subject to broach with the brutish man.

"You follow Caprice Lansing on Instagram. Please tell us how you know her and how you started contact with her?"

"I have no idea who the hell that is. I follow her on Instagram? I am not surprised. I follow almost seven thousand people on Insta. I am probably following her because we have mutual friends and the site suggested I follow her. How should I know? That's the only reason I can think of. Who is she? Why do you ask?"

Tommy interjected, "She is a recent homicide victim."

The detectives were hoping to see some telltale reaction from August but his expression remained calm and devoid of emotion. They learned in the academy that a large part of police work was following your gut instinct. Both of the detectives were coming up empty with this character.

Cosette spent the remainder of the day glued at her desk. She was searching for anything she could possibly find about Mr. Winters. She discovered that he had an identical twin named Alex. The brother lived in Ashland, Oregon. Unlike August's checkered police records, Alex's behavior was closer to that of a monk's. The only thing on his record, to date, was a single speeding ticket. Cosette had a feeling the elusive twin could end up being a wealth of information. Just then, Frank entered the office with a young lady in tow. Cosette estimated her to be in her early thirties. She had thick, black hair which fell into soft spirals to her shoulders and her eyes were expressive and the color of rich, dark chocolate. Her pale eyebrows, while well groomed, did not quite match her caramel coloring. The lady's smile lit up the room and genuine happiness was reflected in the sparkling of her dancing, luminous eyes. Her bright green jumpsuit and arm stacked with silver bangles gave her a trendy, polished vibe. Frank cleared his throat and spoke.

"Cosette, I would like you to meet Octavia Washington. She has several years of law enforcement experience and has been kind enough to agree to help us out here while we are investigating the serial killings."

The ladies shook hands and Cosette instantly liked her new coworker.

"Welcome aboard, Octavia. It's a pleasure to meet you."

"The pleasure is all mine, Cosette. I'm excited to be here. I know we have our work cut out for us. I did some research on the recent murders and it is certainly a doozy of a case."

She agreed with the soft spoken lady and the trio sat down at the table. Cosette caught Frank and Octavia up on the latest events.

"Tommy and I interviewed August Winters earlier today. He's a shady character, to say the least. I did a little online research of him. He has an identical twin who lives in Oregon. Unlike August, he is squeaky clean. I was going to give him a call later this afternoon and see if he can give us any helpful information about his brother."

"I have an even better idea," offered Frank. "If years in law enforcement have taught me one thing, it's that a phone call is no match to actually having a face to face interview. Phone interviews are okay if there is no other option but an in person interview will give you information that the other, less personal method can't. Face to face meetings allow you to see their body language and facial expressions. Plus, your time together is much more focussed than over a phone. Why don't I book you a flight to Oregon for first thing in the morning? I think it will be worth our while."

Cosette was excited by the prospect. She really enjoyed her new career. Each day taught her more valuable tidbits about investigative and interview strategies. An hour later, she received her flight confirmation. Spencer would stay with Luke for the two days while she was away. She missed them both so much. Cosette's time had been spread thin with her new, budding career. Lately, she went home, slept, showered and returned to the office again. There was little time for anything else. Thankfully, Luke was patient and supportive.

Cosette was engrossed in her case notes as the jet ascended into the overcast sky. The aircraft shook from the turbulence the foreboding, thunder clouds caused. It was a quick flight. She barely had time to finish her ginger ale before the plane began to make its descent into the Ashland Municipal Airport.

Upon arrival, Cosette rented a white, two door compact car and headed to her boutique hotel located in the heart of Ashland. She was speechless as she drove towards the idyllic town. It was cradled at the base of the Siskiyou and the Cascade Mountain range. Once in town, the boulevards had plenty of restaurants, theaters and art galleries to choose from.

Cosette's room was tastefully decorated. She felt like she had entered another world when she was in her suite. The room's private deck overlooked the bubbling, scenic Ashland Creek. After freshening up, Cosette drove to Alex Winters' home. Tommy had been able to reach him and he was available to be interviewed today. Frank wanted to be certain that he was willing to meet Cosette before she flew to his home-town. Luck had been on their side because not only was Mr. Winters willing to talk, he was actually eager to have a discussion about his twin. His home was a short distance from Cosette's hotel.

A distinguished gentleman with a room brightening smile answered the front door. Cosette found it difficult to believe that he was the identical twin of the appalling August Winters. He escorted her to a tidy seating area and offered her a cup of coffee. Normally, she would decline beverage offers from someone she was interviewing but Alex was so welcoming that Cosette happily accepted his offer. Within moments, he returned with a steaming mug of coffee. She needed the caffeine jolt. It was going to be a long day for her.

During the interview, Cosette determined that although the twins shared similar features and bone structures, Austin had lived a hard life and was mean spirited which is what caused a striking difference in their current appearances. The interview covered all aspects of August's life. They discussed their childhood first. Alex painted a picture of his twin which was volatile and unstable. In fact, August had even been violent with him on many occasions.

"I have not seen my brother in almost five years. I've learned that I am better off without his toxicity in my life. At most, we send each other an occasional text, maybe about once or twice a month."

"Are you aware that he was in a year long relationship with a lady named Roseanne Buchanan?"

"He mentioned her to me a few times. Their relationship ended abruptly. At least, that is what my brother told me. I am just trying to figure out why the police are so interested in August? Did he do something?"

"There have been a few murders in the South Lake Tahoe area lately." Before Cosette could continue speaking, Alex interrupted, "And you think my brother is the killer?"

"We are still early on in the investigation. At this point, we are interviewing any and all people who have close ties to either Roseanne Buchanan, Patsy Goodwin or Caprice Lansing."

"Wait! Did you just say Caprice Lansing?" startled Alex.

"Yes, are you familiar with her?" Cosette knew that August followed Ms. Lansing on Instagram, so, she was particularly eager to learn why Alex recognized her name as well.

He was visibly shaken.

"August used to talk about her all the time. They dated for about nine months a couple years back. She left him and he was crushed."

Cosette felt goosebumps crawl up and down her arms.

"Your brother claimed he had no idea who she was even though he follows her on Instagram."

"Well, he's a liar! Don't believe a word that comes out of his mouth. I hate saying this about my own flesh and blood, but I could absolutely see him being a killer. He treats me better now, but in our childhood he was brutal with me. August was a terror. Our parents were at their wits end about him. They even put him in a home for juvenile delinquents for a while. The facility could barely even deal with him."

"Thank you for all of your information, Alex. Here is my business card. If there is anything else you can think of, anything at all, regardless of how minor of a detail it may seem to be, please don't hesitate to reach out to me. You have been very helpful."

"The pleasure is all mine, Cosette. Hey, since you are still in town until tomorrow, I would love to show you around. Maybe we could have dinner tonight?"

Although Cosette felt flattered by the handsome gentleman's attention, she was deeply in love and committed to Luke.

"That is such a kind offer, Alex, but, unfortunately, I have a great deal of paperwork to do today."

Getting the hint, Alex bid the striking detective goodbye.

20

Cosette returned to Virginia City with enough information about August Winters to fill an entire file cabinet. Frank pored over every word of her notes and determined, "I don't believe in coincidences. The chances that anyone dated two of the three victims is astronomical. Especially, since one of them lives over four hundred miles from here. Heck, there's a higher chance a volcano will erupt in Nevada. Plus, Mr. Winters has the motive. Both women dumped him and he was full of fury. How Patsy Goodwin plays into the equation, I haven't pieced together yet. Here's the thing, no significant DNA was found at any of the crime scenes. So, lifting one of his cigarettes or a disposable cup won't do us a lick of good. But, I think it's critical that one of us tails him. He claims he never leaves the house. Well, he had to leave his residence in order to put a rat in Ms. Buchanan's mailbox. So, we already know he is being untruthful about that. Also, he blatantly lied when he claimed not to know who Ms. Lansing was. His story has more holes in it than Swiss cheese."

Frank continued, "Tommy, why don't you start following him? If he as much as sneezes, I want to know about it. Octavia, please head on over to August's place and see if he will allow another interview. We need to analyze what his reaction is when he finds out that we talked to his brother and you tell him that we know he was in a relationship with Caprice Lansing. I wouldn't call first, Octavia. Just show up. The element of surprise will work in our favor. Cosette, I would like you to meet Nicholas Trident. He requested a meeting with our department for today, after lunch, in South Lake Tahoe at the Second Cup Cafe. It is located on Emerald Bay Road."

It was an unusually hot, sultry summer day as Cosette made her way to South Lake Tahoe. She cranked the air conditioning in her car to full blast. Her throat felt dry and she popped open a can of lemonade. The liquid soothed her throat and cooled her down. The sweltering heat was creating a mirage of reflecting pools of water on the road ahead. The sun was a ball of fire clinging to the atmosphere in the cloudless, turquoise sky. As she entered the town, the streets were close to vacant. The few brave souls Cosette spotted were meandering on the sidewalk, nursing iced drinks and clothed in wide brimmed hats and tank tops. She pulled into the coffee shop's nearly empty parking lot and entered the business. The rich scent of coffee beans and other confections wafted at her. Cosette was a few minutes ahead of schedule. Nicholas wasn't there yet.

She chose a two person table in the corner. Moments later, Mr. Trident breezed in. Despite his five star smile, Cosette could see the despair in his eyes. She noticed that he still wore his wedding ring, a thick, classic, gold band. He greeted her warmly and took a seat. After a few pleasantries, a server came over to take their orders. Both decided on iced coffees. The idea of drinking a hot beverage during a heat wave was far from appealing.

"Thank you for meeting me here. I want to tell you how much I appreciate the countless hours you have all put into trying to locate my wife. I miss her more than ever but it has helped with my anxiety somewhat to know that I have people on my side trying to find her and that I am doing everything I possibly can for her. It broke my heart when the police just gave up in the past and said she had taken off on her own voluntarily."

Cosette filled Nicholas in on all of the information she had gathered to date. She assured him that she would continue to work every angle to discover where Amber was. Nicholas felt reassured by their meeting.

The server came back over to see if they needed anything else. Then she placed the check on the table. Both Cosette and Nicholas reached for it but Nicholas was a second ahead of her. He insisted on treating her. He reached in his pocket and pulled out a wallet. Cosette was startled by what she saw. His wallet looked identical to the stingray wallet Luke had discovered a while ago in the backyard of his lake house. There was even a white, elongated oval design on the front of it. Nicholas noticed her stunned expression and inquired, "Is everything ok?"

"Yes, I just noticed your wallet. It's lovely. Where did you get it from?"

"Amber gave it to me shortly before our wedding. It is made of stingray skin. It's very special to me."

Cosette's pulse was racing. She pulled herself together and simply responded, "Wow, it is a beautiful wallet."

21

Octavia knocked on Mr. Winters' cabin door. She heard a man's voice growl, "What the hell do you want now?"

"Excuse me?It's Octavia Washington from the Reno Police Department."

A larger than life man creaked the door open and peeked out.

"Well, I'll be darn! I assumed it was one of those other two pesky detectives who dropped by recently."

He stepped out and the detective saw him magically transform from the Grinch on his grumpiest day into a beaming teddy bear. He reminded her of one of those characters in cartoons whose eyes blow up in size when they are smitten. If Octavia wouldn't have witnessed the change with her own eyes, she would never have believed it.

"Sweet Jesus! There is a God, after all!"

"I beg your pardon?" inquired Octavia.

"Ms. Washington, you have got to be the most ravishing creature I have every laid eyes on. To what do I owe the pleasure of your visit?"

Octavia had heard reports from Tommy and Cosette that the gentleman before her was more vicious than a Great White Shark. To her amusement, he was closer to a lovestruck school boy. He attempted to neaten up his hair with his fingers and he tugged self consciously at his rumpled shirt.

"May I come in and ask you a few questions?"

"Heck, do ducks fly? Your every wish is my command. Please come and have a seat. May I get you a cup of coffee or maybe some tea?"

"That is very kind of you to offer but I just had some."

Ms. Washington interviewed August for about an hour. He admitted that he had been in a relationship with Caprice Lansing and that he had previously covered it up because he knew that it would look suspicious that he was in a relationship with two of the murder victims.

"Listen, Octavia. I know I'm rough looking. I am the first guy law enforcement will want to pin things on. The truth is, I heard that Roseanne had been killed because it was local. It was hard to miss on the news. However, I had no clue that Caprice was killed also. She lived all the way on the other side of our state. We hadn't had contact in a while. Nothing about her death was ever posted on social media. I freaked when your coworkers told me that Caprice was murdered. I froze up and, yes, I lied that I didn't know her. I can tell you one thing for sure. I'm not crazy about either one of my exes but I sure as heck wouldn't kill them. That just isn't who I am."

During the span of the interview, August must have told Octavia that she was the most gorgeous person to have ever inhabited this planet at least four times. She couldn't help but feel charmed by the man's antics.

"Mr. Winters, if you can think of any other information that might help, no matter how small or insignificant it seems, please feel free to call or email me. Here is my business card."

"Does that include calling you and telling you that I miss you already three minutes after you drive away?"

Octavia couldn't help but chuckle.

"No, sir, business related discussions only."

"Aw, shucks. That's fair, at least for now." August winked shamelessly.

Tommy positioned himself in a discrete spot near August's property. His vehicle was hidden behind shrubbery. In this dense forest, there had been many hiding spots to choose from. He felt confident that Mr. Winters would not detect him here. The stakeout was uneventful for the first few weeks. His newspapers would pile up for several days before he would stumble out to the front of his driveway and collect them. Occasionally, a grocery delivery truck would bring supplies to him. August wasn't kidding when he told them that he rarely left the house. Tommy was appreciative of the much needed reprieve he got when one of his coworkers would take over the stakeout while he went home, cleaned up and rested.

Cosette was at the office, deep in thought about the case when, without warning, Luke and Spencer bounded in.

"Oh my! You two sure are a sight for sore eyes. What a surprise!"

"We have come to whisk you away for a bit. You have been working nonstop. I'm hoping your schedule will allow for a little break?" Luke asked hopefully.

"I think I can manage that," giggled Cosette. "Where are we going?"

"We can't tell you. It's a surprise." Spencer chimed in.

"Now you've got me in suspense."

The trio headed to Luke's car. Cosette couldn't fathom what they were cooking up but she was intrigued. Just shortly outside of Virginia City, Luke pulled into Tommy's driveway. Cosette laughed and said, "Why on earth are we at Tommy's house?"

"You'll just have to wait and see."

Tommy exited his home and greeted them with his usual warmth and enthusiasm. Cosette determined from the look on Tommy's face, that he was indeed involved in their scheme as well. He escorted them through his tidy home and directly into the shaded, manicured backyard. What Cosette saw almost stopped her heart. Eight adorable Rhodesian Ridgeback puppies and their proud mother raced towards them. Cosette had been so involved in their case, that the puppies had temporarily slipped her mind. She lowered herself to the ground and embraced the tiny balls of energy. They were all so precious. One, in particular, caught her attention. This puppy was a little shy but her soulful eyes melted Cosette. She immediately felt a connection. Spencer darted over and asked to hold Cosette's dream puppy. Her son looked enraptured. He had been begging to have a dog of his own since he was about three years old. Another one of the puppies untied Spencer's shoe laces.

Tommy announced that the exact pup Cosette had felt the immediate connection to was indeed the puppy he had put aside for her.

She still needed to be nursed for two more weeks but then they could take her home. This would give them time to get the necessary puppy supplies and pick a name for her.

22

Weeks passed and local law enforcement was not getting any closer to identifying the serial killer. Tensions were high and the detectives felt discouraged. Solving a case was not as easy as the crime shows on television made it appear. Cosette reminded herself that these shows had to neatly tie up an investigation in the time slot the show was allotted but that was not how real life worked. Initially, dozens of tips about the "Water Bearer" killer had been called in on a daily basis. Every one of those tips had to be researched and followed up on. The tips from well meaning citizens had now dried up.

Cosette continued to work every angle in hopes of discovering what had happened to Amber Trident. So far, she had not progressed in uncovering the truth about the woman's mysterious disappearance.

It was Friday evening and Cosette was finishing up some tasks before she headed home for the weekend. The sharp ring from her cell phone shattered her concentration. It was from an unidentified number.

"Hello, Cosette DuPont speaking."

She heard a deep, husky voice state,

"I'm going to finish what he started."

Cosette froze and her heart lurched. She attempted to conceal the raw panic in her voice.

"Who is this?"

A horrible, evil sounding laughter erupted from the caller's throat. Then the phone went dead.

Cosette reached for the Smith & Wesson revolver in her bottom desk drawer. Her palms were cold and clammy. She wanted to tell herself that it was probably some kids doing a prank call but she knew the deep voice she had just heard could only belong to an adult male. She placed the gun in her waist pack and headed cautiously to her car. Nothing in her surroundings appeared out of the ordinary. Luke was expecting her for dinner at his place. She headed straight there and was relieved when she was able to fold into his warm, awaiting arms. Her fiancé always made her feel safe and loved unconditionally.

They sat by the pool with a pitcher of margaritas and chips piled into a cactus shaped basket. It paired perfectly with the plastic, jalapeño, guacamole container. They were always very careful not to have glass by the pool. When they were nestled together on the outside sofa, Cosette told Luke about the daunting phone call she had received. His eyes filled with horror and he was momentarily at a loss for words.

Trying not to alarm his fiancee but still wanting her to be aware that this could be a serious threat, he fumbled for the perfect words to say.

"I am sure it is a meaningless threat but we need to be extra vigilant just in case. The first thing I thought when I heard what the caller said to you is that he was referring to when the serial killer kidnapped you but, thank goodness, you were rescued before he could physically injure you."

Cosette had thought the exact same thing. The killer back then had intended to end her life. Luckily, she was rescued before he was able to do that. He was now sitting in jail for the rest of his life. Did the caller mean that he was going to end her life?

This was the first time since Cosette had graduated from the police academy that she had truly feared for her safety. She would need to report this daunting call to Frank, Tommy and Octavia as soon as possible.

Cosette put her cares to the side and enjoyed her evening with Luke. After a while, he handed her a pocket calendar from 2023.

"What is this?" Cosette inquired.

"I am pretty sure that you and I still need to set our wedding date. I am counting the minutes to become your husband. I figured that since you have had time to settle into your new career, we might finally be able to decide on one. Please pick a date? Any date which calls to you."

Cosette beamed with excitement.

"How about tomorrow?" Cosette teased.

"I would love that but I know it is important for you to have our relatives and closest friends there. But, if you want to elope, I'll be all over it," added Luke.

"You're right. I have been dreaming about getting married at St. John's Church along Tahoe's west shore. They book up quite a ways in advance."

Cosette picked up the calendar and thumbed through the different months. One date in particular caught her attention.

"How about Saturday, April 29th?"

"I love it," agreed Luke. Why don't we call St. Johns and if they have April 29th available, let's set it. Then we will need to decide on our reception place."

The couple could barely contain their excitement. Sunshine flooded Cosette's soul.

"Yip! Yip!" A high spirited puppy interrupted the quiet night. Trixie, their puppy, bounded onto the pool deck. Her emerald green collar reflected in the moonlight. It was hard to believe that Cosette had been a bundle of nerves just a couple hours ago. Her family was like poultice for her heart and soul. Spencer and Romeo joined them moments later. They enjoyed a hearty supper and swam until bedtime.

23

The killer had been very patient, waiting for things to settle down. He knew his intelligence far outranked all the fools working on his case. Sure enough, his case was turning as cold as the lousy meals his Aunt Betty used to make for him. He wasn't stupid. He knew that killing someone while law enforcement was actively watching, would have been a grave mistake. He got a slight satisfaction from watching Roper, his boa, feast on live bait. Of course, watching his pet kill was not enough to keep him calm for very long. He needed to murder again. It would be impossible to hold off for much longer. The time was almost here.

Tinsley was back at work. The casino scheduled weekly support groups for any employee who needed extra help processing Roseanne's tragic homicide. Every Wednesday evening, Tinsley would file into a conference room and bare her soul to the familiar faces from her workplace.

The room was completely packed this evening. Tinsley felt the fatigue from her brutal shift tugging at her eyes like a toddler clinging to his mother's apron but she was insistent about going to the group therapy session, nonetheless. She knew she needed the extra support.

Peter, Melissa, Tyler and Gabe were dispersed throughout the room. Tinsley opted for the seat next to Peter. She adored all of them but felt especially close to and at ease with Peter. The hour long session passed by in the blink of an eye. Tyler was particularly somber this evening. At times, he was even tearful. Tinsley hadn't been aware that he was particularly close to Roseanne. Her friend had never mentioned Tyler to her. Near the end of their meeting, Gabe asked if he could have everyone's attention.

"I know we are all heartbroken over the passing of Roseanne. I felt it was time to turn my grief into something productive. I am setting up a fundraiser in hopes of raising award money for anyone who is able to identify who the local serial killer is.I would like to encourage employees from our casino and anyone else we can enlist to take part in a bike-a-thon. The goal is to get people to sponsor us for each mile we bike along our route. The proceeds will go to increasing the reward amount. We need to catch the monster who ended our friend's life. I would really appreciate all of your support. Let's do this for Roseanne."

The room erupted into applause.

While Peter appreciated Gabe's touching gesture, he was sickened to see Tinsley's impressed expressions while gazing at the hunk of a man before them. Gabe had been a thorn in Peter's side since day one. Every time he thought of him, so much acid churned in his stomach that it could burn a hole in the hull of a ship.

Peter needed to see his supervisor for a brief meeting after the support session. Tinsley was eager to go home and did not want to wait for him. Her fatigue was overwhelming at this point. She had purchased a taser since Roseanne's untimely demise. It was bright pink in color and was even adorned with a handful of crystals. Who said she couldn't be safe while also being stylish? She was scheduled to start a self defense class in three weeks.

Tinsley entered the gloom of the night as she drove her car home. Her townhouse lot was filled to capacity. As a result, she had to parallel park one block away. The crescent moon above cast very little light. The night was pitch black, partly overcast and quiet. She marched at a steady pace along the blackened sidewalk. A distinct clap of footsteps behind her were rapidly approaching. Tinsley trembled inside. She sped up but the foreboding footsteps increased in speed as well. The steps were heavy and insistent. The person clearly had a mission. Panic surged through her. The branches above swayed and looked like menacing, grabbing claws. She was about a hundred steps away from her home when she heard her name being called. She looked in the direction of the voice and could see Peter standing under the streetlight at the entrance to her building. At the exact moment that Peter called, the footsteps behind her retreated and then vanished. Tinley's eyes began to tear. She knew, without a doubt, that she was being pursued by someone who meant to harm her. She collapsed into Peter's arms and her tears flowed like the steady stream from a water pitcher.

A startled Peter held her close. She told him what had happened. He pleaded with Tinsley to let him sleep on her sofa so he could keep an eye on her. He hadn't told her this but he had been fearful for her safety ever since Roseanne's homicide. His life would be over if anything every happened to her. Tinsley happily accepted his offer. They walked up to her front door. Peter spotted something on the doormat and gasped. He reached down to pick it up. What he retrieved, sent shock waves through both of them. It was another stingray skin wallet!

Tinsley called her mother, Fiora, and filled her in on her horrifying night. Fiora was naturally concerned and made a plea.

"Darling, please let me reach out to my dear friend, Frank Munro, from the Reno Police Department. He is as good as one can get when it comes to investigating and solving mysteries. I would like to have him assign one of his employees to keep an eye on you and get to the bottom of who was stalking you tonight. Please, it would make me feel so much better. At the very least, someone could monitor you when Peter is at work and you are alone at home."

Tinsley was touched by her mother's generous offer. She was hesitant to give up her independence, however. Sensing what her daughter was thinking, Fiora quickly added,

"They can keep an eye on you in a way that isn't intrusive. Please, Tinsley?"

Tinsley agreed to her mother's kind suggestion.

"I have been on edge since Roseanne's death. Between Peter staying with me and someone from the law enforcement monitoring me, I may start feeling a little more at ease."

Fiora was relieved by her normally stubborn daughter's acceptance of the offer.

24

Monday morning arrived too soon for Cosette's liking. After leaving a voicemail at St. John's Church, she brewed a strong cup of coffee and settled in the office at Luke's home. He was having interviews this morning to hire two bartenders at his restaurant, The Watering Trough. Her fiancé's restaurant was a hot spot in Virginia City. Luke had worked hard to ensure that it ranked among the top establishments in the county.

Spencer had already left for school. Her son had been a little anxious this morning because he had to give a brief presentation on Grizzly Bears today to his class. Cosette had practiced with him repeatedly over the weekend. Her son was particularly fascinated to learn that the hump on a Grizzly Bear's back was in actuality a muscle and that the bears enjoyed dining on moths. His speech came complete with photographs of the powerful and beautiful animals.

She had an optimal vantage point of the town below from the expansive window. Soon after, and without warning, what appeared to be a wall of brown air stretched high and was rapidly approaching. It was a sand storm. This type of weather was not uncommon in Virginia City. It crawled noiselessly over the garden's hedges and towards Cosette's window. The dust twirled above the infinity pool and across the lawn. It reminded her of a ghost. The trees looked like veiled brides huddling together in the dust.

Cosette became engrossed in her work. At one point, her eyes travelled to the far right edge of the property. A movement in the dusty air caught her attention. She froze. A large, menacing figure stood there, cloaked in a loose fitting, hooded overcoat. Cosette rubbed her eyes to ensure that the combination of fatigue and the sand storm weren't playing tricks on her. By the time she refocused, the dubious individual had vanished. Luke's property stood on several acres and there were no immediate neighbors. Somebody wouldn't just happen upon the grounds. She was convinced that she had, in fact, seen an intruder in the backyard. Fear consumed her. Cosette didn't want to disturb Luke. He had a packed schedule today. Cosette knew that her fiancé would drop everything he was doing to run home to her. She inspected all of the doors and windows on the ground level to make sure that they were locked and bolted. Then she set the home security system.

The shrill of Cosette's cell phone startled her. She had been a jumble of nerves since she spotted the suspicious person. Her voice crackled anxiously as she answered.

"Hello?"

"Cosette, it's Frank."

Relief flooded every inch of her body.

"I got a call this morning from a good friend of mine, Fiora Banks. Her daughter, Tinsley, was close friends and a coworker of Roseanne

Buchanan. Tinsley is convinced that someone was stalking her the other day when she was heading back to her home. Her mom is very worried about her. Would you mind going to Tinsley's home in South Lake Tahoe this afternoon? Why don't you interview her and see if she can give us more information about what she saw or heard when she was being followed. Who knows? Picking her brain might even give us some valuable information about Roseanne's homicide. I don't want this case to go cold, under any circumstances."

Cosette jotted down Tinsley Banks' address and was just about to jump in the shower to get ready for her meeting when her phone clanged again. This time it was the secretary from the church. She confirmed that they did indeed have the 4:00 p.m. time slot on April 29th available.

"That is wonderful news!" exclaimed Cosette. We would love to book that time. With that, Luke and Cosette finally had their eagerly anticipated wedding date set.

Now we just need to find a reception place which is available to start at about 5:30 p.m on that date. That way our wedding day will move seamlessly from the ceremony directly into the reception. Maybe I can swing by some venues in the Lake Tahoe area after I finish my meeting with Tinsley.

After freshening up, Cosette pulled on a scarlet red jumpsuit, black strappy sandals, a sterling silver necklace with a roadrunner pendant and silver, hoop earrings. Then, she punched in Tinsley's address into her trusty GPS and was off on her day's assignment.

25

It was Faith Gunder's day off from her vet tech job at Shores Emergency Vet Clinic. She uncharacteristically slept in until almost 10:00 a.m. It was a well deserved rest. She had been putting in double shifts at work for eight days straight. Faith checked her phone as she was sitting down for a Belgium waffle breakfast at her cramped kitchen table. Fifteen texts had been delivered to her in just the last half hour. It was a group text with a handful of her best friends. Jessica was coordinating a last minute get together at the local roller skating rink.

The friends had been going to the Silver Skate since they were all in elementary school.

The skating place and Bob's Bowling Shack were two of their favorite hang out spots.

Faith confirmed that she would be there at the designated time. She dialed her dear aunt's number. Aunt Ruth picked up immediately.

"Faith, I was hoping you'd call," her effervescent aunt exclaimed. "How have you been, my darling niece?"

"I'm pretty good, Auntie. You know, the usual. Working for what feels like endless hours. I love the animals so much but it's the demanding owners I could do without. I finally have a day off today and tomorrow. I am going to meet Jessica, Dawn, and Christina at the rink later today."

"I worry about you working so much. You are wearing yourself out. And how on earth can you meet anyone special if you never have a moment to take it easy? Sweetheart, you will be twenty-five in just a handful of months. I am getting impatient to become a great aunt to your little babies. It is time to find Mr. Right."

Faith was used to her aunt's pressure to settle down. She knew that she meant well and just wanted her niece to be happy and in love.

She didn't relish that Ruth regularly brought up her single status but her aunt had always been one of her closest confidants so Faith put up with it.

"I promise that I'll work on it," assured Faith.

After the call, she watched two episodes of her favorite show, Below Deck. She had to flip the television off when a rat was shown scurrying across the ship's deck.

In general, Faith considered herself a fairly fearless individual. The only thing on this earth which scared her so much that it would send her shrieking and crying for the hills is if she saw a rat. Her family was poverty stricken as a child. They would rent motel rooms by the week. She remembered one place just outside of Topeka, Kansas where they stayed for the entire summer in her early teens. Whenever she would get up during the night to use the restroom, she would see the vile vermin scatter to the corners of the bedroom. Once, she even found one floating in the toilet. Just the thought of rats would make her feel nauseous and engulfed in terror.

Stop reliving these heinous memories. It will only freak you out. Today is about relaxing and having fun.

As soon as she calmed down, she starting dolling herself up for her get-together. She wore snug fitting jeans, a vibrant purple halter top, and long socks. The length of the socks was key. Faith had discovered from an early age that if she wore short socks, her ankles would hurt, she'd develop blisters and she would suffer for days to come. She put two coats of midnight black mascara on her velvety, thick lashes, powdered bronzer on her dainty nose and chiseled cheek bones, coated her razor thin lips with a lavender shade of gloss. For the final touch, she tussled her long coils of chestnut brown hair up into a low, carefree looking ponytail. Faith surveyed herself in front of her mirrored closet door. The outfit emphasized her sculpted physique and enviable tapered waist.

Before she left, she filled a water bottle with tonic water and vodka. The Silver Skate didn't serve alcohol so Faith and all of her friends always came prepared with pre-filled containers. She took a swig of the drink.

I may as well start the party early. I need to make this rare day off count.

The fog had finally burned off as Faith left her condominium. She entered the blinding sun and meandered to her car. Golden strands of sunlight radiated off of the sidewalk and the surrounding lawn. The sky was a cloudless, blazing teal blue color. A light breeze stirred the surrounding plants and flowers. The pleasant aroma of the next door ice cream shop filled the air with its sweet vanilla and strawberry scents.

Faith tossed her trendy three knotted cord tote bag onto the front passenger seat, slipped on her knock off Chanel sunglasses and flipped the radio onto a popular, local rock station. The high volume of the music caused the entire car to pulsate.

With all of the car's windows wide open, Faith made her way to the Silver Skate. She was the first of her friends to arrive. Since it was a Monday afternoon, she assumed that they would, more or less, have the rink to themselves. Making one final inspection in the rear view mirror of her hair and makeup, she scooped up her bag and water bottle and sauntered to the front counter to pay her admission's fee. Then she waited on a heavy piling, zebra print sofa in the entry area. Faith could remember sitting on this same sofa here when she was barely six years old. Not wanting to waste a minute of her precious day off, she eagerly took another swig of her potent drink. Faith was already feeling the calming effects of the liquid as her three best friends arrived.

Her friends burst like fireworks on the 4th of July into the establishment. The Silver Skate was a second home to all of them. Justin Bieber's "Stay" was blasting over the speaker. The friends worked their way to the lacquered, wooden rink. The D.J.,Aaron, was a scruffy looking, underweight man. What he lacked in appearance he more than made up for with his warm personality. He was friendly, genuine and he was a loyal friend to Faith. The girls had all attended kindergarten through high school with him. He greeted them with a broad, sincere smile and turned the volume up even higher for their enjoyment.

The skating session lasted for two and a half hours. At one point, they headed over to the snack station. The girls filled up on corn dogs and curly fries loaded with ketchup. Aaron timed his break so he could sit with them. Since the group of friends were the only skaters at the rink, it was easy for him to coordinate his break with the intermission.

The group huddled together at a corner booth. Faith complained about her grueling work schedule. Aaron chimed in, "You should apply here. We are looking for a manager. The pay is pretty good. The hours are not nearly as rough as what you have now and the benefits are excellent. Plus, we could see each other all the time, an added bonus."

Faith was intrigued by Aaron's suggestion. As much as she enjoyed working with animals, the hours were slowly but surely wearing her into the ground.

"That is a great idea. Would you happen to have an application I could fill out?"

"You bet I do. One minute, I'll go and get it from the office."

Aaron came back with more than just the application. He also brought the owner of the business, Mr. Bailey, with him.

Faith had known the kind, salt and pepper haired owner since she was a child. He had been a fixture at the skating rink for decades. Mr Bailey confirmed with Faith that she was actually interested in the position. She emphasized that she would very much like to apply.

"I'll tell you what, I get this is a little last minute but would you like to meet for an interview when this skating session is over? Then, you can send me your C.V. over email later this evening."

Faith was delighted. This could be just the change she needed. She was sick of feeling tired and run down constantly.

The girls continued to skate and when the session concluded, Faith dutifully reported to Mr. Bailey in his office. The interview went perfectly, partly because she had known the gentleman for most of her life. He offered her the job on the spot. Out of respect to her current employer, she would need to give him two weeks notice, but, after that time period, she would be available to work as the manager at the Silver Skate. Faith was brimming over with excitement as she called Aunt Ruth on the drive home.

26

Cosette called Luke during the drive to Lake Tahoe in order to fill him in on their confirmed wedding date. He was overcome with excitement and he was eager to get the reception scheduled as well. She promised that if her meeting with Tinsley didn't go until too late, she would still visit a few potential venues in that area.

She rapped on Tinsley's door and within seconds a charismatic, striking, young lady answered. She could easily have won first place in a Miss America competition. Her warm and bubbly personality reminded Cosette of a ray of sunshine.

Tinsley guided Cosette to the seating area of the family room.

After some pleasantries, Cosette proceeded with her questions.

"Mr. Munro tells me that you were very close to Roseanne Buchanan. I'm so sorry for your loss."

"Thank you! This whole thing has felt like a never ending nightmare. Roseanne was like a sister to me. I still can't believe she is gone."

"Do you know of anyone who might have wanted to harm her? Any enemies, someone she had a feud with recently, ex boyfriends?"

"Roseanne was very well liked by everyone. I know she had a creepy ex-boyfriend named August Winters. He was pissed off when she dumped him. Roseanne was scared of him. He harassed her after the break up. She was in tears one day at work because he had left a dead rat in her mailbox. She talked about him less often right before her death. He had slowed down on harassing her. Roseanne didn't seem as frightened by him near the end of her life."

"Have you ever met August Winters?"

"Oh sure, he would often hang out where we work, the Crystal Waters Casino, while they were together. At the time, I thought he was pretty cool."

"Why was that, Tinsley?"

"He had a great sense of humor. We would all be in stitches when he was around. However, he had a pretty bad temper too. I heard him screaming at the top of his lungs at poor Roseanne often. Then he got even nastier to her when she ended things."

"Frank told me that you believe you were being followed a couple of days ago. Could you tell me about that?"

"It was very scary. I had just come back from work. I stayed a little later than usual because I went to a grief support group. I couldn't park in the lot here because it was full. So, I parked my car about a block away. The night was pitch black. I have no doubt that I heard distinct footsteps trailing me. When I sped up, so did the person behind me. Thank goodness that my friend, Peter, was waiting for me at the entrance to the building. If not, I am convinced I would have been assaulted or worse. When my friend called out my name, it seemed to alert the person following me, and he or she backed away. I believe Peter saved my life. Since then, I have been so scared that Peter has even been staying at my place when he isn't at work. He works at the same casino as I do."

Cosette was jotting all of the information down. Then she continued the interview.

"Tinsley, has anything else unusual happened since Roseanne's homicide. Have you seen any other suspicious people around you, received any strange phone calls or social media messages? Is there anything else that comes to mind?"

Tinsley thought for a moment and then she leapt off of her seat exclaiming breathlessly, "Oh, wow. I almost forgot. There is something else which seemed out of the ordinary."

She reached into the coffee table drawer, pulled out two items and handed them to Cosette.

Tinsley detected Cosette's audible gasp as she recognized the stingray skin wallets. Goosebumps erupted all over the detective's skin and she suppressed a shiver.

"Where did you get these from?"

"Not just once, but twice, someone has left a wallet on my doormat."

Cosette inspected the wallets. She was certain that they were identical to not only the wallet which Luke had found at the lake house but also to Nicholas Trident's wallet. *What was the connection?* Cosette wondered. Nicholas had received his wallet from his wife, Amber. She was now missing. If she had any doubt before that Tinsley was in great danger, those doubts had vanished into thin air. This young lady was definitely at high risk of becoming one of the killer's victims. At the conclusion of their meeting, Cosette arranged for an officer from the South Lake Tahoe Police Department to come immediately and guard the entrance to Tinsley's apartment. Cosette felt that the young lady was in imminent danger and should not be left unattended.

After the officer arrived and Cosette had wrapped up her meeting with Tinsley, Cosette headed to a stunning, ten acre private resort located directly on the western shore of Lake

Tahoe. She gave herself a self guided tour of the grounds.

A large, glass door opened to an outdoor terrace which was only a few feet from the lake's edge. It was an ideal location because the covered terrace would allow the reception to continue at this location regardless of the weather on their wedding day. The end of April was often sunny in this area but the weather was far from guaranteed. She didn't want to bet their wedding day on the weather conditions. Cosette collected pamphlets from the venue and headed to a lakefront hotel and spa next.

She was impressed with this location from the moment she arrived. The crystal blue waters splashed against the open air ballroom. A gorgeous koi pond was nestled in the far corner of the venue. The mountain views were incredible. Cosette had heard that the culinary team at this location was unbeatable as well.

Cosette's final stop was to a quaint inn. The site overlooked the lake on one side and the snow tipped mountains on the other. This venue also included an outdoor or indoor option depending on the wedding day's weather. The inn featured a cozy lantern and candle lit ballroom, expansive lawn and a private boat dock.

Jeanie, a dynamic, middle-aged lady, noticed that Cosette was surveying the property. The onsite wedding planner approached her and gave her a synopsis of all the reception options which they had available. Cosette fell in love with the site. Jeanie checked the inn's schedule and confirmed that they did have the evening of April 29th still available. Cosette made an appointment to return with Luke and Spencer for the following weekend. She could, of course, not make such a monumental decision without her family involved in the process.

27

Faith loved her new job at the skating rink. Her hours were not as grueling as they were at her former job. She loved that she could sleep in. She didn't have to report to work until 1:00 PM and her shift normally ended at around 10:00 p.m.

A romance had sparked with her long time friend, Aaron. He wasn't necessarily her type physically but she loved how he made her feel; relaxed, happy and confident.

Aunt Ruth was euphoric when she heard about their budding relationship. Aaron was happier than he had ever been before. He was perpetually walking on air. He finally admitted to

Faith that he had been secretly in love with her since sophomore year of high school. Never in his wildest dreams, did he think she would end up being his girlfriend. His shift ended at 8:00 p.m. every night. Faith would work the last two hours of her shift and then she would go over to Aaron's house. They would have take-out food and binge watch Netflix.

Fortunately, today was extra busy and the last two hours breezed right by. It was Faith's responsibility to lock up at the end of the night. She did her final checks to ensure that all the electronic devices had been shut down and then she entered into the crisp, stormy night. Typical of the season, there had been thunder storms throughout the day. Electrical storms were common place in her blissful, alpine town.

The half moon was entirely shrouded by the heavy cloud coverage.

"Clap!" The thunder tore through the sky and reminded Faith of a piece of jet black paper getting mercilessly ripped in half. The illumination from her iPhone guided her down the rickety steps and to   the cover of her awaiting car. The umbrella she had been holding was now turned inside out from the intense wind. Attempting to stay dry was useless. She placed it under her arm, unlocked her car and scrambled inside for shelter. Her pants were already soaked down to her skin. Droplets of rain dribbled over her cheeks and onto the collar of her ruby red raincoat.

Turning on the ignition, she let out a sigh of relief as the heater was beginning to do its magic on her frosty skin.

Faith was just about to put the gear into reverse when she heard something so horrifying that her entire world came crashing down around her. A breathless, deep voice sounded from the backseat. His guttural tone hissed,

"You are going to do exactly as I say. If you listen to me, you will be ok. I don't want any trouble. Got it?"

Sheer terror climbed along her spine. Her blood turned to ice. Faith's lungs were rummaging for the air necessary to scream. She was paralyzed, unable to exhale, unable to speak.

"I brought some friends for you," chuckled the demonic being in the most insane voice Faith had ever encountered.

She detected the faint sounds of hisses, chirps and squeaks. Rats were in the car and, in fact, several of them!

Faith was all too familiar with the sounds rodents made. She had been plagued by the vile creatures for a large portion of her childhood. Currently, they were in the back seat with her assailant. She could detect the signature scratching noises their paws made as they approached her.

The unidentified man, still in the backseat, put a rope around her torso which pinned her arms and made them unusable. She felt the rodents scurrying around her neck and over her head, their nails digging into and piercing her delicate skin.

The man feigned kindness and said mockingly,

"I know everything about you, Faith. When will you women smarten up and not have such set daily schedules? You made it very easy to stalk you. I know that your birthday is on March

18th. You adore your spinster Aunt Ruth and you have an ungodly fear of rats. I just wanted to make the last moments of your life extra special. So, I brought some of your childhood pets along. Rats! Your life is about to end!"

His laughter was deafening, louder than a pack of hyenas on the African Savanna.

Those were the last words Faith heard before the rope was fastened viciously around her neck. For the final touch, the killer callously threw the Aquarius necklace on her chest and poured the contents from a water bottle all around her corpse. His victims were normally left by a body of water. He was unable to make that happen with Faith at this location. Therefore, the very least he could do was bring liquid with him.

The killer exited the car and whistled merrily off into the stormy night.

28

The detectives all received a text late the following morning stating that their presence at an emergency meeting at the South Lake Tahoe Police Department was requested for 1:00 p.m. that day.

Cosette had spent the morning monitoring Tinsley's townhome. She was hidden on a side road, kitty corner from her building. From this vantage point, she was able to see if anyone entered or exited the building. Frank was convinced that Tinsley could very well be a target of the "Water Bearer" serial killer. As a result, monitoring Ms. Banks had become one of the highest priorities of law enforcement. By keeping a watchful eye on her, not only could they potentially save a young woman but they may also be able to crack the case wide open and discover who the elusive killer was. While Cosette was sitting in her car, she was able to research which stores the mysterious stingray skin wallets were sold from. So far, she had determined that the identical wallets could be purchased on Amazon and at two other local stores. She would need to get back to the task at hand after the meeting. Once the next officer arrived to continue monitoring Tinsley's home, Cosette bookmarked all the information she had gathered and proceeded to the police station.

A grim and anxious looking chief of police commenced the meeting at the standing room only station.

"The serial killer has struck again. A young woman, Faith Gunder, was found unresponsive in her vehicle in the parking lot of the Silver Skate. The same signatures were present at this scene as with Patsy Goodwin, Caprice Lansing and Roseanne Buchanan's crime scenes. Again, a necklace with an Aquarius zodiac pendant was left on her chest. Faith was also strangled. One aspect of this crime scene was much different than the other three scenes. This victim's vehicle contained almost a dozen live rats."

An audible gasp was heard throughout the room.

Sutter Munro continued,

"We are not yet clear of what the significance is of rats being part of this murder scene. The "Water Bearer" has not struck in quite some time. He killed again because he got restless and overly confident. I don't want our town to be referred to as the serial killer capital of the United States! We need to work together, investigate every single angle and finally catch this bastard!"

Sutter dabbed the perspiration off of his brow. The tension in the room was palpable.

"I want every aspect of Ms. Gunder's life looked into. That includes interviewing anyone even remotely connected to her. Scour all of her social media accounts. The rats in her automobile were not domesticated rats, so researching recent purchases from pet stores or feed stores will not do us any good. The killer accumulated the rodents from the wild. See if there is any connection at all with Ms. Gunder to our other victims. I feel it is crucial that we find out what role rodents played in this murder.

He is going to kill again and, my guess is that he will do it soon. This killer is getting cocky. I am giving a press conference in under an hour from now. As you all are aware, it is key we keep a lot of this information close to our vests. Presumably, only the killer knows these details. I don't want it getting out that he leaves a necklace on each victim. At least, not yet. We can't risk enticing a potential copy cat killer or having an individual come forward with a false confession."

After Sutter closed the meeting, each member of law enforcement was assigned specific tasks to tackle. Cosette estimated that there were about seventy people present.

Some of the more tech savvy officers were asked to focus on the social media accounts of the victims or to search records in data bases of each of the victims and all of their family members, coworkers, exes and social contacts.

Others were asked to continue to scour Faith's car and the surrounding area for fibers or genetic material.

The remainder of the officers were assigned to interview witnesses and people with ties to the homicide victims.

Cosette had briefed Sutter that a mysterious stingray skin wallet was left on two separate occasions in front of Tinsley's door, once at Luke's Tahoe residence and that Nicholas Trident had received the identical type of wallet as a pre-wedding gift from his now missing wife. Her task was to interview those closest to each of the victims to determine if they had also received such an item before their tragic homicides.

Her first stop would be to visit Patsy Goodwin's husband, Jeff. He had an airtight alibi for the day his wife was killed. As an attorney, he left their home at about 7:00 a.m. in order to attend a deposition. Patsy was seen leaving the home midmorning by a neighbor. The coroner determined that her time of death occurred during those morning or early afternoon hours. Mr. Goodwin had been in court until 5:00 p.m.

The lawyer never left the courthouse property. Cosette was hoping that he would be able to shed some light on whether his wife had received any mysterious items prior to her death. It would also be an opportune time to question all aspects of Patsy's life such as if she had any known enemies, jealous friends or if she exhibited any usual behavior in the days or weeks before her homicide.

29

Tommy was starting to nod off in his car when he detected movement in the vicinity of August Winters' front door. He had been spending more months than he cared to count, staking out this thud's cabin. The man barely even stepped out of his home and, up to this point, he had never left his property. He watched the eccentric character fumble to his old, mustard colored Lincoln. He looked a little more cleaned up than usual.

Nothing fancy. He still borders on grungy but at least he looks a little less shabby than his usual house attire. I think this might finally be go time, thought Tommy hopefully.

The ancient car started up and a gust of smoke exited the tail pipe as if revolting against finally being moved. As far as cars went, she had an easy life. She barely ever moved and she sat uninterrupted in a lovely wooded grove. This sudden call to duty clearly did not please her. August ran his car for a solid nineteen minutes before he finally started driving. He knew that she needed, rather demanded, that crucial warm up period.

Finally, the elusive Mr. Winters was off and at a speed that made the tree branches shake and the birds fly skyward. Had he been a race car driver in his past? Tommy was up for the task. He considered himself a bit of an aficionado when it came to cars. He raced them and worked on them extensively in his twenties.

He needed to be discrete. The key was to keep August in his sights but not to create suspicion by following too closely.

This was not an easy task. The dirt road in front of him resembled a sand storm in the Sahara Desert due to Mr. Winters' high speed. Tommy trailed him for about ten minutes. August pulled into the parking lot of, none other than, the Crystal Waters Casino.

Now this is getting good, thought the dedicated detective.

August parked and headed into the casino. Tommy was close on his tail. August's first order of business was to dart to the slot machines and order a stiff drink from the alluring cocktail waitress, Tinsley Banks. He seemed comfortable, familiar even, with her. They had some relaxed banter while August ordered drink after drink.

This man feels connected to the murders in several ways. Two of the three women murdered are his ex girlfriends and he even knows some of the casino employees on a first name basis.

Melissa brought August his 4th drink. At this point, his eyes were glazed over and his movements were wobbly. She eyed him like a starving person would look at a prime rib and lobster buffet in Vegas. Tommy observed Melissa whispering something in August's ear. He chuckled and winked at her. She motioned for him to follow her into a supply closet. It didn't take a rocket scientist to figure out what contact sport they were about to take part in. Tommy felt quite confident that they were not going to play Scrabble. August emerged exactly four minutes later. Tommy didn't know whether to feel impressed by the lightning quick session or to feel pity.

I've been vaccinated slower than that, thought Tommy amusedly.

August had a spring in his step and his eyes looked clearer and more alert. With a renewed calmness, he proceeded to the casino's Neptune Swim Center. He entered the humid enclosure, walked searchingly around its entirety and then proceeded to leave the casino. Tommy was watching. He continued to remain undetectable.

Cosette rang on Jeff Goodwin's door. A somber looking man greeted her. She recognized him from the photos she had seen online and at the station. His eyes were bloodshot and he sported dark, prematurely lined, bags under his eyes suggesting many nights of insomnia. He asked Cosette to come into the living room. His movements were zombie-like and devoid of expression or emotion. The room smelled of a tangy, orange citrus air freshener. She had the feeling that Jeff had not aired the home out in weeks and the citrus was his half hearted attempt to make the residence not smell like a sweaty men's locker room. The room looked like a shrine for his deceased wife.

The walls were covered with Patsy and Jeff's wedding portraits and artistic looking collages from their various trips. No matter where Cosette looked, Patsy's haunting eyes seemed to be watching her.

Cosette first expressed her heartfelt condolences. She felt as if speaking to the table lamp would have elicited more of a response. Her heart hurt for this man's obvious pain. They then spoke about how the couple had met, what their relationship was like. Jeff claimed that they had always had an incredible marriage. Battling infertility caused a great deal of stress in their lives but the couple had managed to keep their lines of communication open. He insisted that they had still adored each other up until the very end. Cosette moved into the next phase of her questioning.

"Could you tell me about some of the people closest to Patsy, family members, friends, even acquaintances? Any information would be very helpful for the investigation."

"She was close to her family. Her only sibling, Eliza, was her best friend. They never had conflicts. They got along great. She had a handful of friends here. They hadn't seen each other as often lately. Patsy became more reclusive as soon as she wasn't able to conceive. Every single one of her friends started having babies. It became painful for her to see them."

"Did Patsy have a falling out with any of the people in her life recently?" prodded Cosette.

Jeff closed his eyes and was quiet for a while. The silence probably only lasted for about forty seconds but, for Cosette, it felt like it drew on endlessly. She waited patiently until he cleared his throat and began speaking again.

"Patsy really was a very easy going and likable person. There was one friend she had a quarrel with about a year ago, Lindsey Plantine.

She lives just a block away from us. We would go on couple's dates with Lindsey and her husband, Hank. It was nice. We would have cookouts together and go to dinner at a variety of local restaurants. One day, Hank admitted to Lindsey that he had developed a crush on Patsy. My wife had no idea until her friend came over here in a rage and confronted her. That was the end of their friendship."

Cosette had to broach the next question delicately.

"To your knowledge, did anything ever happen between Patsy and Hank, emotionally or physically?"

"Absolutely not! Hank even told Lindsey that his feelings for my wife were one-sided and they had never behaved inappropriately with each other. I trusted my wife. She wouldn't do that."

Cosette couldn't help but detect some bitterness in Jeff's voice. She documented the other couple's names so she could research the matter further.

"There was one more topic I wanted to discuss with you, Mr. Goodwin. Did Patsy every mention, or did you ever see, any unusual object left at your residence or on your property?"

"No, like what?" he responded.

Cosette may have been a little wet behind the ears when it came to law enforcement still, but she had learned enough to know never to offer this type of information to anyone during an investigation. Cosette restated the question.

"I am just trying to figure out if there were any unusual occurrences before Patsy's death, any strange phone calls or items discovered which didn't belong here."

"None that I can think of."

Cosette then asked if she would be permitted to have a look around his home. He would have had every right not to allow her to. She held her breath. To her surprise, he agreed.

"Go ahead. Nobody wants this monster caught more than I do. Take your time. If you'll excuse me, I have some work to do in my home office."

Cosette thanked him and, before he could change his mind, she began to go systematically through the spacious, modernly appointed home.

She inspected closets, drawers, behind bed frames and even on the underside of tables and chairs. Cosette found items one would expect to find in a typical upper class home, stationary and towels monogrammed with the letter G and his and her home offices. The bathroom cabinets were stocked with Tylenol, Tums, toothpaste and Patsy's prescription for a high dose of Prozac.

The impressive master suite came next on her self-guided tour. The room featured high ceilings. It was adorned in mint green hues. There was a calmness and tranquility to the space. The bed was king sized and overfilled with throw pillows in shades of cream and silver. The elegant, upholstered headboard was the focal point of the room.

Sadness pierced at Cosette's heart as she pondered that this bed had been, at one time, the stage for Patsy Goodwin's dreams. She began to open drawers and look under the solidly built furniture pieces.

Cosette assumed that the room had not changed much since Patsy's murder. One nightstand cradled a masculine looking watch and a Men's Health Magazine. The other nightstand had a delicate, rose printed catch all tray, a lavender scented hand cream and a book about eating well for optimizing chances of conceiving. Cosette inspected the pages of the book to ensure that there weren't any hidden notes or cards in them. There was nothing but a butterfly shaped bookmark.

Then, she pulled open the drawer of the nightstand. At first, the contents seemed almost mundane. There was a thermometer, mints and a box of thank you cards. Cosette peered deeper into the drawer. Wedged towards the back, she spotted a dark object. She reached her hand in and pulled the item from its constraints. What Cosette saw sent shock waves throughout her body. It was a black, stingray skin wallet with a white oblong design on its front. Fear crept along her spine like an icy finger.

Cosette took the wallet and headed to Jeff's home office. As she was walking to him, she detected a slight, rattling sound emanating from the mysterious wallet. Peering inside, she saw an item glinting in the depths. Cosette plucked the shiny object from its confines. Her eyes widened and her hands began to tremble. It was a silver necklace with an Aquarius pendant!

Cosette proceeded to Jeff and asked him if he knew anything about the wallet. He claimed he had never seen it before and based on his reaction when the wallet was presented to him, Cosette believed him. She asked him if she could take the mysterious object with her. To her relief, Jeff consented without hesitation.

Cosette traveled swiftly to the South Lake Tahoe Police Department and reported her discovery to Sutter Munro. He was speechless which was not common place for him. When he finally regained his composure he stated, "We know that the unsettling necklace was left on each of the victims' bodies. One of our victims, Patsy Goodwin, also had the mysterious wallet and the necklace in her home. Nicholas Trident was given an identical looking wallet from his now missing wife, Amber. Tinsley Banks had the same type of wallet left at her front door on two separate occasions. She believes that she is being followed and she has close ties to one of the murder victims, Roseanne Buchanan. Finally, your fiancé discovered a stingray wallet in his backyard. It doesn't take a neurosurgeon to figure out that Tinsley Banks is more than likely one of his intended targets. We need to keep an eye on her. I will continue to have one of our officers monitor her. I can't have another lady losing her life. Also, Cosette, I feel like I need to address the elephant in the room. You were abducted by the last serial killer from our area. I find it extremely disturbing that such a wallet was left on Luke's property. To make matters worse, you told me about the unsettling phone call you received. Please be vigilant and report any more unusual activity to me immediately. We don't want this monster to try and complete the first serial killer's job. These nuts just love to copy each other."

30

Peter had been staying with Tinsley at her townhouse every moment when he was not at work. The two had become inseparable. He had been deeply in love with her for years but his feelings had only intensified recently. The truth was that Peter was scared senseless since the rash of serial killings. He could not bear the thought of ever losing Tinsley or to have anyone harm her. It particularly hit home for him when their dear friend and beloved coworker, Roseanne, was brutally murdered by the monster.

After some initial resistance on Tinsley's part, Peter was sleeping on her sofa every single night. He would dart there immediately after his shift ended. Their evenings would include taking walks along the lake, watching their favorite shows and indulging in a combination of nutritious, tasteful home cooked suppers and scrumptious restaurant meals. Often, Peter would pick up dinner for them on his way home from work.

Tonight started out as similar to any other night. Peter picked up takeout at neighborhood Thai food restaurant. Tinsley had an insatiable craving for Chicken Pad Thai. She continued to deny it but Peter was convinced that she outright snorted and guffawed on two separate occasions when she had recently devoured her Thai meal.

Peter let himself in with the house key. He loved spoiling Tinsley. He didn't even want her to deal with dishes or any of the clean up.

"Tinsley, I'm home."

That was something he had wanted to say to her for years but ideally under other circumstances. He longed to be her husband. He ached for her but he couldn't put his selfish needs before her happiness. She was his top priority.

Tinsley greeted Peter with open arms and a wide, beaming smile.

"I brought some sustenance, your favorite, Thai food."

"Peter, thank you so much. I haven't eaten in hours. I'm starving."

Peter could never understand how Tinsley could eat like a lumber jack but never gained an ounce of weight. He doled out their meals and they enjoyed a relaxing evening together.

When they were fully sated, they retreated to the sofa and watched Golden Girl's reruns. Usually, Tinsley giggled endlessly during this sitcom. Her mood was different tonight. She seemed somber, even fearful. Her shoulders slouched and she continuously draped her head onto Peter's shoulders. When they had finished the 4th episode, Tinsley announced that it was time for her to go to bed.

Peter wished her a peaceful night with sweet dreams and she retreated to her room. He got settled on the sofa. He even had a weighted blanket and fleece sheets to make him extra warm and cozy. He set his alarm and was just starting to drift off when he felt a soft hand on his shoulder. His eyes had adjusted to the darkness and as he looked up, he saw Tinsley standing there. Her hand was reaching for him. Without saying a word to each other, she guided him to her bedroom.

A few hours later, upon awakening, Peter's first thought was,

Tell me this wasn't just some glorious dream!

Fearful to discover that, in fact, it had been only a dream, he hesitated to open his eyes. He squinted and peeked cautiously out of one eye. Sure enough, Tinsley was laying just a few inches away from him, still deep in slumber.

I can't blame her for sleeping. We were up until the early morning hours, he thought, feeling self satisfied as he stretched his arms languidly. Peter had been praying to reunite with Tinsley ever since their untimely break up years ago. His love for her had somehow only managed to deepen over time. She was all he needed, everything he had ever wanted.

Since there wasn't a lot of talk between them during the night, he was scared senseless that Tinsley may have just intended it to be a one night tryst. He wanted so much more. Eventually, his ultimate dream was for her to become Mrs. Tinsley Novak.

31

The evening cast long shadows on the sidewalk as Cosette exited the police station. The sky was cloudless and ablaze with tangy orange and crisp yellows shades. The warm breeze swayed the leaves of the surrounding Japanese Maples. She detected the subtle floral and smoky notes floating from the neighborhood coffee shop. It awakened her senses and gave her a much needed jolt of energy. It had been an endless day and it was far from over.

Cosette needed to pay Lindsey and Hank Plantine an impromptu visit. She figured the chances of finding them at home were optimal since the average work day had already ended.

The detective arrived at their address and was impressed by the clean lines and geometric shapes of the modern, pleasing to the eye, home. Cosette rang on their doorbell and she heard footsteps inside. After a minute, she rang again. A lady, Cosette estimated to be in her thirties, opened the door cautiously and peeked out. She was gaunt, sported mid length, dirty blond hair and had a somewhat bulbous nose.

"What can I do for you?" she inquired somewhat impatiently.

Cosette introduced herself and Lindsey motioned for her to come inside with a hint of reluctance. The ladies sat in the sunroom on a floral, upholstered sectional. A glossy coffee table was laden with books about home decorating and national parks of the United States. A geometric area rug completed the look of the room.

A man, Cosette assumed was Hank, peered into the room.

"Hank, come on in. This is Detective DuPont. She just wanted to ask us a few questions."

The husband's face blanched and he looked visibly shaken.

He entered and slumped into the wicker chair. Hank was a large man with strong muscles, a broad neck and penetrating, gray eyes.

"What is this all about?" he demanded somewhat gruffly.

Cosette explained that she was investigating Patsy Goodwin's murder. She detected an audible gasp sound from Lindsey.

"Linsey, why don't I start with you? What was your friendship like with Patsy? Did you continue to have contact with her up until the end of her life?"

The couple looked uneasily back and forth at each other.

"Patsy was one of my best friends. Then, my pig of a husband destroyed that."

Cosette was taken aback by the wife's blunt words.

Hank injected, "Cut it out, Lindsey. You just love blaming me for everything!"

"We both know that Patsy and I would have stayed friends if you hadn't gotten all hog wild for her and then you were even stupid enough to confess it to me."

Cosette knew it was time to take back control of the interview. If she didn't, they would only continue to bicker back and forth endlessly.

"Let's just have one person speak at a time, please. Hank, is it true that you developed feelings for Ms. Goodwin?"

"Yes, but that sort of thing can happen. We hung out with both Patsy and Jeff all the time. Patsy was a great lady. It was hard not to fall for her, especially since my wife can be…difficult and moody often."

"Was Patsy aware of your feelings for her? Did you ever take your relationship with her to a physical level?"

"Patsy had no idea about my feelings for her until my blabber mouth of a wife had to go running over there and report it to her."

Lindsey stood up and began shaking her arms in anger. This was the most difficult interview Cosette had encountered so far in her short career.

By some miracle, Cosette was able to calm Lindsey down long enough to continue the questioning.

"And, we never did anything physical," insisted Hank. "Patsy was like a saint. She was very devoted to Jeff. She would never have messed up their marriage. Besides, all she ever had was babies on the brain."

Cosette continued to question the couple on every topic she found could be even slightly useful in discovering more about the deceased lady. Neither of them were aware that Patsy had possession of the strange wallet, or, at least, they claimed not to. She thanked them for their time and began driving back to Virginia City. She was about a half hour into her drive when she received a call. To her surprise, it was Hank.

"Cosette? I need to talk to you. I told Lindsey that I forgot to get something at the grocery store as an excuse to leave the house and call you."

The detective's interest was piqued. She considered driving back to meet Hank in person but she figured that if he gave the excuse of running to the store, his time was limited and he would need to return home soon.

"What may I help you with, Mr. Plantine?"

She could hear the gentleman's voice crackling. He clearly was on the verge of tears.

"I wasn't honest with you earlier. There was no way I could admit certain things with my wife sitting there. The truth is that Patsy did have an affair and she was in love."

Cosette was confused.

"With whom?"

"With me! We had an extramarital affair for about five months. They were the best months of my life. We were very much in love. Then Patsy felt guilty about our relationship and she ended it. Lindsey and Patsy's friendship continued. I was still able to see her when we went out on double dates. It was better than not seeing her at all. A couple months later, after a few drinks, I stupidly admitted to my wife that I had a crush on her. A crush is a huge understatement. She was the love of my life. I never admitted to Lindsey that we had an affair. My wife raced over to Patsy's house in a rage. Their friendship ended and, of course, Jeff permanently froze me out after that."

"Patsy called me a few days after Lindsey's outburst and told me that if she ever saw me again, it would be too soon. She said she would never forgive me for admitting my feelings to Lindsey."

"I have never gotten over losing her. I mourned the end of our romantic relationship and then I mourned all over again when she was viciously killed."

The detective thanked Hank for coming forward with this information. As Cosette disconnected their call, she decided that she would need to further investigate Mr. Plantine. He was a jilted lover and he had admitted that he had a substantial falling out with Patsy. Of course, it was in Hank's favor that he had called Cosette and had admitted that he had an affair with the deceased lady. The detective appreciated his honesty. Still, she had a feeling that Mr. Plantine could end up being a key player in this murderous puzzle.

32

Finally, Tinsley emerged from her slumber. Peter had been patiently waiting for her to awaken.

"Good morning, sleeping beauty."

She smiled and moved in closer to his chest.

This must be a good sign. I doubt she would nuzzle up to me if she regretted last night.

Peter could feel her heart beating against his skin. He sighed and was overcome with relief and happiness. He didn't want to push it and ask her too many questions about where their relationship currently stood. He figured that all of his burning questions would get answered naturally over time.

The bike-a-thon for Roseanne, which Gabe had spearheaded and organized, was scheduled to take place this afternoon. Gabe called Tinsley and asked if he could swing by. Peter knew it was critical to contain his jealousy. It would not be a good look if Tinsley noticed that he was upset by the Don Juan's visit.

The doorbell rang and Peter darted to open it. Gabe seemed startled that Peter was at Tinsley's residence.

"Hey buddy, I didn't expect to see you here."

"Oh?" retorted Peter more agitated sounding than he had intended to. Tinsley interjected, greeted the visitor warmly and asked him to come in.

"What brings you here, Gabe?" inquired Tinsley.

"I just thought I'd swing by and talk to you before Roseanne's bike-a-thon later today. I have been having problems getting enough sponsors. I know you have a big social circle.

Are there other people you can think of who would be willing to sponsor?"

Tinsley contemplated the question and then responded,

"I actually have some friends from high school who I can approach before the event starts. I will get right on it. I bet I will be able to drum up some extra business, especially since it is for such a good cause. So many people loved Roseanne."

Gabe thanked her and said that he needed to get to the starting point of the event to begin setting up booths. He turned one last time and scowled at Peter. Tinsley seemed clueless about the interaction the two men had just shared.

I hate everything about that man. Has he been working out more? His shoulders were practically too broad to get through the front door. He is just a wide necked baboon. I also despise him because he is acting like some kind of hero about setting up the bike-a-thon. He is a phony and I sure as hell will never let him interfere in my relationship with Tinsley.

Cosette, Octavia and Tommy were engaged in a working lunch together at the office. Ever since Octavia had interviewed August Winters, their office resembled a floral shop. He regularly sent bouquets of flowers and succulents to the object of his affection, the lovely Octavia. She attempted to reject the deliveries but August would intentionally use a variety of flower companies and he would instruct them to leave the floral masterpieces in the courtyard without making their presence known.

Cosette wasn't sure whether to feel amused or concerned. The last note which August attached to an impressive bouquet of tulips stated, "God spent six days creating the universe. On the 7th day, he perfected your beauty." August transformed from a classless brute into a charming gentleman whenever Octavia was around. Cosette would not have believed it, if she had not witnessed it herself.

Just then, Frank waltzed into the office.

"Folks, let's have a quick pow wow. As you are all aware, the bike-a-thon being held in Roseanne Buchanan's honor is taking place in

just a few hours from now. Here is the bottom line. It is very common for the killer to show up to these type of events. They get off on seeing the pain their murders caused friends and loved ones. I would like all three of you to take part in the fundraiser. I have bikes and helmets for you in the courtyard and I already submitted your paperwork. Position yourselves along different points of the path. Keep your eyes and ears open for any behavior that just feels off."

*Cosette, Octavia and Tommy reported to the starting line of the bike-a-tho*n. Hundreds of cyclists were present. The energy and festive feel in the air was infectious. Most of the participants were wearing bike shorts, t-shirts and windbreakers. The sky was cloudless, sparkling and dotted with Mallard Ducks, Canadian Geese and Mountain Chickadee's. The lake was vodka clear and statue still. The weather was behaving exceptionally well as if it wanted to honor Roseanne in a special way.

Tommy was an avid cyclist. The trio had agreed that he would be near the front of the bicyclists. Octavia would cycle around the middle of the crowd and Cosette would putter along towards the back.

Gabe Patterson, the organizer, delivered a speech to the crowd. He thanked everyone for their support and he was visibly overtaken with emotion as he briefly discussed Roseanne's life. Then he blew his whistle and the crowd was off.

Cosette made sure to stay near the back of the line. Her eyes darted among her fellow cyclists for the duration of the ride. Unfortunately, she did not witness any unusual behavior.

Thus far, nobody at the event piqued her interest. Once Cosette passed the finish line, she spotted a variety of concession stands. She passed a table of refreshments. Some of the booths sold bicycle related merchandise. One booth specialized in sunglasses. They were even holding a raffle for two complimentary tickets for a dinner cruise on the Tahoe Queen.

All three of the detectives circulated among and monitored the crowd. The line for the water bottles and juice boxes snaked around the block. A toddler threw a raging tantrum when his mother didn't get him an ice-cream cone. Cosette rubbed her temples. She was beginning to feel the start of a headache. The heat felt blistering on her shoulders. She had always been religious about sunscreen. Her beloved Aunt Suzette tragically passed away at the young age of thirty-eight due to the skin cancer, Melanoma. Cosette will never forget the suffering her aunt endured. She vowed then that she would always be vigilant about protecting her skin.

The three detectives continued to survey the event. Just when Cosette believed that they would turn up empty for clues from this event, she saw something that piqued her interest. A man, she estimated to be in the second half of his twenties, was in the process of purchasing a t-shirt at one of the registers. He fumbled in his pocket and then pulled out a wallet, a black stingray skin wallet with a white, oblong design!

Cosette signaled to Tommy and Octavia that she had detected something unusual. The trio decided that Octavia and Tommy would continue to monitor this event while Cosette would trail the man with the suspicious wallet.

The gentleman stayed at the event for another half hour. He ordered a fried chicken meal with a large coke and then sat at one of the picnic tables. He seemed famished. He gulped the meal and appeared to barely chew its contents. Finally, he guzzled his soda and stood up abruptly. The man collected his bicycle and rode out of the event. Cosette shadowed him for about ten minutes. Then, he pulled into a cottage driveway. The structure was relatively small, stood on one level and was constructed of logs. It was cocooned in a grove of redwood trees. Sunlight was unable to filter in due to how heavily forested the area was. A small front porch, overlooking a pond, jutted out from the quaint home. The gentleman parked in the carport adjacent to the cottage and entered the house.

The detective texted Tommy and Octavia from the side street. She needed them to bring her car and laptop to her. Within twenty minutes, two cars came rolling down the quiet lane. Tommy delivered Cosette's car. Then he jumped into Octavia's car and the duo headed back onto the road to return to their Virginia City office.

Cosette positioned her vehicle so that she was out of view from the mystery man. She then pulled out her laptop and, within minutes, she was able to identify the owner of the cottage. Tyler Herman, a twenty-eight year old parking attendant employed at Crystal Water's Casino. Cosette recognized his online photo as the man she had been trailing.

Hmm, he works at the same casino as Roseanne and Tinsley. That is highly suspicious that a coworker of two of the victims has one of those wallets. What are the odds?

The detective started to dig deeper online. He had received the cottage he currently lived in from his father, Leonard Herman. Tyler had a couple of brushes with the law in the past. His indiscretions were petty theft and a DUI.

Next, Cosette reviewed his social media platforms. He followed Roseanne and Tinsley on Instagram. She figured that since he worked with them, following both of the ladies was hardly unusual. The detective scoured the social media accounts of the other murder victims. At first glance, Tyler was not following them on any of the platforms, at least not by his true account. Cosette was well aware that it was not uncommon for individuals to set up bogus accounts to stalk and catfish others. She could not rule out that he wasn't involved in something like that.

The detective was so engrossed in her online searches that she became slightly startled when she saw Tyler's car emerge from his driveway. The distraction from texting on his cell phone allowed Cosette to remain undetected as he passed by.

Stalling for thirty seconds, she finally pulled out and began to tail him. One of the first things the instructors taught her in police academy was how to follow somebody while remaining imperceptible. Keeping one's distance, refraining from running stop signs or traffic lights and, most importantly, never follow your suspect until after they begin to move. Mentally reviewing the tips for tailing, Cosette proceeded.

Tyler progressed along at an excessive speed. He was a hazardous driver. After a few minutes, he pulled into the parking lot of El's Hideout, a neighborhood bar. It was a hot spot for the town's residents. On Saturday nights they even had mechanical bull contests. Luke had won first place in the contest a few months ago.

Tyler slid his BMW into a compact spot, surveyed himself in the rear view mirror, and then headed into the watering hole. Cosette looked down at her clothes. She was not expecting to frequent a bar today. She was still wearing her bike shorts, sneakers and a magenta colored tank top. She combed her hair and applied some cherry lip gloss. It was to her benefit that she worked as law enforcement at the Reno Police Department. She was not known by the locals in Lake Tahoe. As a result, it was much easier for her to blend in and do her investigative work.

Cosette entered the establishment. Upon scanning the crowded room, she spotted Tyler. He was sitting at the bar, accompanied by a man and a woman. The detective moved next to where they were seated and motioned for the bartender. She ordered a rum and coke. The bartender was a vibrant, friendly man. Cosette gauged him to be in his forties. He had a receding hairline and his long forehead only managed to emphasize his rapidly dying hair line. The gentleman's eyes were warm, round, and hazel colored. His generous lips naturally curved upward into an inviting, genuine smile. He began to make small talk with her.

"I am Seth. Welcome to El's Hideout! I don't believe I have ever seen you in here before. I am guessing that you aren't a local?"

Cosette had already figured out the full story she would give if she ended up being questioned about her identity while pursuing Tyler.

"It is nice to meet you, Seth. I'm Jenna. I live in Roseville. I came into town for the bike-a-thon in honor of Roseanne."

Cosette could see Tyler and his friends leaning towards her and listening intently to her conversation with Seth. Her statement about being in town for the bike-a-thon had clearly captured their interest.

"Oh, wow! You have come quite a long way. Did you know Roseanne?"

"I did. We went to high school together. I am devastated about her death. Is there any talk around town about who the killer could be?"

"There is some talk. She had a crazy ex, August Winters. Some people think he killed her, but, who knows?"

Seth excused himself and walked away to take another client's order.

"Hey, Jenna, I'm Tyler. We couldn't help but overhear you talking. We were at the bike-a-thon too. In fact, my buddy here, Gabe, was in charge of the event. This is Melissa. She is a cocktail waitress at the Crystal Waters Casino. All three of us work there."

Cosette seated herself on the bar stool next to them, reminding herself that for the duration of the conversation, she was named Jenna from Roseville.

Seth returned with her rum and coke.

"Well, it is nice to meet you. I sure worked up a thirst after all that bike riding," exclaimed Cosette as she took a sip of her cocktail. The group laughed and Gabe made a toast to their beloved Roseanne.

Then, the small talk began. Gabe told Cosette that he was the lead guitarist in a garage, punk rock band. As he continued to speak, Melissa climbed onto Tyler's lap and was blowing and giggling in his ear. Gabe became distracted by her overt display of affection. He seemed agitated and stated to Tyler,

"What's up? This was meant to be our guy's night out. Melissa wasn't even supposed to be here. You've barely talked to me once tonight."

Tyler retorted,

"Chill out, buddy."

Gabe sprang off of his chair and left the bar in a huff. An awkward silence ensued. Tyler focussed in on Cosette and said,

"Jenna, I am sorry for his outburst. Gabe is a good guy. When he drinks, he tends to get angry and moody."

Cosette figured this could be the perfect entry into finding out more about all of them.

She made another quick mental note to herself, that for the sake of this group, her name was Jenna. She was new in law enforcement. Pretending she was somebody else was not something she was accustomed to.

"I wonder if some of his agitation is connected to Roseanne's death?" pried Cosette.

"It hurt him, for sure," responded Tyler.

"Were they close?" persisted Cosette.

"Yes, somewhat. They got along well."

"Were you close to Roseanne?" pushed the detective.

"Yes, she was great. We all miss her every day."

Melissa nodded in agreement.

"Listen," continued Tyler, "Melissa and I have some unfinished business we need to deal with. We are going to have to wrap up our little shin dig."

Melissa giggled suggestively.

Tyler pulled out his distinctive stingray wallet and retrieved his credit card. This was Cosette's ideal opportunity to inquire about the ominous wallet.

"That's an interesting wallet? Is it leather?"

"I have no idea," he responded gruffly.

"Where did you get it from? I would love to get my dad one just like that," fibbed Cosette.

"I can't even remember. I've had it for a long time."

Tyler was clearly irked by their conversation. He settled the bill and bid Cosette goodbye.

The detective was left alone in the bar. Her mind was spinning. She knew she needed to head over to the police department and report her findings from today.

33

Fatigue took over. His brain was constantly tortured. His existence was a life of agony. The only reprieve he ever experienced was the deep rest during slumber. Even then, he was usually plagued with nightmares.

She dove into the fresh, crystal-clear lake. It was summer vacation. They had just enjoyed a foot long tuna sandwich with all the fixings. The sky was a brilliant blue and cloudless. The sun hung hot and unforgiving in the atmosphere. It almost seemed to taunt the fair skinned. Four hungry seagulls flew overhead, waiting to devour the remnants of their lunch. His sister pulled herself back onto the boat. They were eager for dessert. Rocky Road ice cream with caramel topping and marshmallows were featured on this afternoon's menu. This was the day which had changed him forever. What started out as a special summer outing turned into a day of indescribable self discovery. An entire world had opened up to him, a new passion was born.

After feasting on dessert, his sister retuned to the crispy depths of the lagoon in her pink, polka dot bikini. Her only jewelry was a simple, silver, heart pendant necklace. Her dish water, blond hair was tied up in a ponytail. At first, she was relishing her afternoon swim. Soon after, the scenario changed. His sister's pretty face look distressed. Her brows knitted and her fragile body gasped for every last bit of air. She gulped down water. Her arms fought to reach the surface. A few lingering bubbles of air escaped from her mouth and floated to the top of the lake.

He awoke with a jolt. Perspiration was traversing his crinkled forehead. The bedroom was pitch black aside from a small light illuminating Roper's enclosure.

He dreamt of that summer day from so many years ago often. It was a day which had changed the course of his life. Pleasure and horror were both words he could use to describe his feelings about his sister's demise. It was an interesting cocktail of emotions.

There's no better way to numb my feelings than by having a nice, strong shot of booze.

He traversed through the darkness over to his liquid anesthesia. It had been his savior more times than he could count. The gasoline strength liquor seared his parched throat.

I am starting to spiral out of control. In the past, after I killed, I felt sated for quite a while. Now, I am starting to feel restless even hours after a kill. Ms. Tinsley Banks is slowing pushing me over the brink of insanity. Do those pesky detectives not know that I am fully aware that they have been assigned to keep her safe. They are a bunch of idiots. They will slip and mess up. They always do. I can't get sloppy. This is how some of the serial killers I idolize eventually got caught. Ted Bundy and Jeffrey Dahmer are perfect examples. They got greedy. Most of them are brilliant but their impulses destroyed them.Their arrests can't be in vain. I must learn from my predecessors. We are a team. I need to make them proud and continue their mission.

34

Cosette reported to the office the following morning. Frank had scheduled an urgent staff meeting. Tommy and Octavia were already seated at the table. It was unusual for Cosette not to arrive first at the office. She had been burning the candle from both ends and slept through her alarm this morning. Fortunately, Tommy had already brewed a strong pot of coffee.

Frank breezed into the room with a gentleman in tow.

"Folks, I want to introduce you to James Burton. He just graduated from the police academy in Las Vegas and he is relocating to

Reno. I have asked him to help us out for a while since we have been inundated with work ever since our area has been dealing with a serial killer. Tommy, I would like it if he could shadow you for a couple of weeks so he learns the ropes."

James had the look of someone just embarking on a new career. His eyes were glowing and he looked eager and full of excitement. He was a handsome man. Standing at 6'4", his sun streaked hair, golden skin tone and sculpted physique all hinted of an active and fit lifestyle. His piercing blue eyes and chiseled features only added to his intimidating good looks.

"Thank you so much for letting me help out with your investigation!" beamed James. It has been my lifelong goal to go into law enforcement and I am very happy to be here. Please don't hesitate to let me know if there is anything I can do to lighten your work loads."

Cosette instantly liked him. She generally had a strong intuition about people. She believed that he would be easy to get along with.

Once they were all assembled around the conference table, Frank commenced the staff meeting.

"An interesting new development happened and I am going to need your help. Sutter informed me that August Winters' mother, Jennifer Winters, contacted him. She has end stage pancreatic cancer and she is in a hospital in Switzerland. She told him that she needs to speak to a detective about something related to the rash of killings in our area. He tried to get the information out of her over the phone but she insisted that she wanted to speak face to face with someone. Sutter told me that she sounded very weak. We need to move at lightning speed at this point. He believes that she may feel more comfortable speaking to a female detective. We can't have her backing down in the last minute and not telling us the information. Cosette, would you be willing to travel to Switzerland and interview Ms. Winters at her bedside?"

Cosette was honored that she would get sent on an international assignment so early in her law enforcement career.

She responded, "Consider it done. I would love to meet with her and hear what she has to say. With a little luck, her information could end up cracking the case and help us to catch this vicious killer."

Frank continued, "Thank you. I knew you would be up for the task. I will arrange for you to fly out tomorrow morning. Sutter will let Ms. Winters know that a detective is coming there to meet with her. I am not a betting man, but it seems pretty obvious that what she has to tell us is probably connected to her son, August. Tommy, please continue to keep a close watch on Mr. Winters. We can't have the killer strike yet again."

35

Tinsley stretched and reached her arm out to embrace Peter. There was nothing but empty space in the sheets next to her. Then she recalled that he was spending the day visiting his father at his home in Battle Mountain, Nevada. It was an adorable gold mining town located about four hours away from South Lake Tahoe. He had invited Tinsley to come with him but she had to work a shift in the afternoon.

Peter and Tinsley had become inseparable. They were together, more or less, every waking moment. She would miss him very much while he visited his father. Tinsley had fallen more deeply in love with him than she ever knew was humanly possible. He was her universe and the best part was that he felt the same way about her.

Putscho jumped up on the bed and pushed his chin against her wrist, disrupting her love struck thoughts. He serenaded her with a chorus of purrs. She sighed and with a smile thought,

Life is good. Things sure have turned around for me. I am excited to spend every day of the rest of my life with Peter.

Her eyes became heavy and she drifted off into a brief nap.

A knock at Tinsley's door startled her and interrupted her slumber. She pulled herself out of bed and tip-toed to look out of the peephole. A teenage girl was standing there holding boxes of cookies. Tinsley was not in the mood to deal with hearing a sales pitch. Besides, she had reached her dream weight. She was not about to thwart her efforts by having those delectable temptations in the house.

After the uninvited visitor left, Tinsley knew it was futile to try to go back to sleep. Plodding into the restroom, she brushed her teeth, while the shower water was heating up.

Tinsley's shower time served as a treasured ritual for her. It somehow managed to be both energizing yet, also calming. The steaming water pelted her scalp, face and shoulders. The soothing cascade made her feel similar to when Peter embraced her with his strong, protective arms. She longed to stay here all day but, unfortunately, life was waiting.

As Tinsley emerged from the enclosure, hot water vapor poured out of the glass shower and formed tiny droplets on the mirror.

Her reflection was entirely obscured because of the thick steam. Feeling impatient, she rubbed a clearing on the mirror so she would be able to begin applying makeup. As her eyes adjusted to the still semi-obscure image, she saw the outline of a large figure cowering behind her.

But, nobody is home except for me!

The figure emerged from the darkness of the corner of the bathroom. Terror sealed Tinsley's throat. Panic engulfed her. Her face felt flushed and her stomach cramped. Her muscles shook and twitched. Then her world went entirely black.

36

Cosette was given all of her flight information. She was scheduled to depart out of the Reno International Airport and land in Zurich, Switzerland. Her flight was leaving first thing the following morning.

Cosette called Luke and told him the exciting news. She knew he would be particularly excited since he was 100% of Swiss heritage. Her fiancé's response was even more enthusiastic than she had anticipated.

"Switzerland, of all places? Can I please go with you? We could do a side trip to visit my grandparents and other family members."

Cosette was not about to pass up an opportunity to travel to Switzerland with the love of her life. They made the necessary arrangements. Luke was able to get the same flight itinerary as Cosette. Her mother delightedly agreed to stay at Luke's house to watch Spencer during their absence.

Peter had spent a wonderful day with his father. His dad was one of his best friends. He always enjoyed when they spent time together.

Peter made a point of visiting him for the annual "Armpit of America" festival. The town of Battle Mountain was often referred to as the armpit of America ever since a 2001 Washington Post article dubbed them as such. The citizens embraced this designation and even poked fun at themselves. The town held a yearly festival sponsored by Old Spice. Peter's favorite event was the deodorant toss.

As much fun as he had with his father, he still missed Tinsley ever minute of the day. He could not stand to be away from her.

He drove back to her home in eager anticipation. He pulled into the designated parking lot of the townhouse and smiled when he saw Tinsley's car. He loved her dearly but parking was not one of her strong suits. She had a tendency to park lopsided. It was not uncommon for her to unintentionally park in two spots. People would get infuriated until they saw her. Tinsley's charm melted even the most irate drivers.

Entering the home, Peter called out excitedly,

"Honey, I am home."

He loved saying that every time he returned to the townhouse. He had been dreaming of being able to come home to her for as long as he could remember.

Peter was met with complete silence.

Maybe she is napping or has her earbuds in.

"Tinsley, are you here?"

He entered their bedroom and saw that her phone was on the nightstand. Her purse was in its usual spot, nestled off to the side of the bed. After inspecting the rest of the house, concern began to niggle at him.

If she had gone on a walk or picked up food she would have her phone and her purse with her.

Peter picked up her phone to see if he could look at her calendar. Perhaps she met a friend or had an appointment within walking distance? He didn't know her password, so, he was limited in what he could discover. However, he was able to tell that she had been receiving texts throughout the day and had not retrieved them yet. A text from her mother had been sitting there unread since this morning.

His concern developed into complete panic. Something was wrong. Tinsley had been scheduled to work a four hour shift at the casino earlier today.

Peter called one of her supervisors, Matt, praying that he would tell him that Tinsley had indeed worked her shift. He had no such luck! Matt said that she had been a no show. The boss had repeatedly tried to reach Tinsley. He had been unable to get a hold of her. Matt seemed more concerned that he had been short staffed than about Tinsley's safety.

Peter drove in a state of panic to the police department. Sweat was forming on his furrowed features.

Why did I leave Tinsley alone today? He mentally berated himself. He had been a fool. If something were to happen to her, his life would be over. He drove his car into the first parking spot he found and shot like and arrow into the police station.

A ginger haired receptionist, styled in a crisp, mint green pantsuit, greeted him warmly. Despite her alert appearance, the emptied, extra large, take-out coffee containers told a different story. She was clearly attempting to give herself a jolt of energy.

"How may I help you?" the receptionist inquired.

Peter, feeling short of breath from his extreme anxiety, blurted out,

"My girlfriend is missing. I need to speak to an officer immediately."

"Of course, Officer Evans is available. Follow me, please."

The receptionist escorted him down a long, poorly illuminated hallway, to the officer's desk.

A muscular, bald headed gentleman with soulful, dark brown eyes greeted Peter and asked him to have a seat. After some brief introductions, Officer Evans probed, "What brings you in today?"

Peter explained in a cracked, nerve-laden voice,

"My girlfriend, Tinsley Banks, is missing. I am close to losing my mind. I went to visit my dad today for a day trip to Battle Mountain. She was supposed to work her shift at the Crystal Waters Casino for a few hours this afternoon. That is why she couldn't come with me. When I got home she wasn't anywhere. Her car was in the lot connected to our townhome. Her cell phone and keys were at home. The worst part is that she never showed up for her shift. She has never skipped out on work. That just isn't like her at all. We were good friends with Roseanne Buchanan. Twice now, someone has left a stingray skinned wallet at her front door. I am worried something horrible has happened to her."

Generally, law enforcement did not heavily investigate a missing adult until twenty fours hours from the point of when they were reported missing. Officer Evans, however, heard Peter telling him information which was deeply concerning. It was common knowledge among local law enforcement that a stingray skinned wallet was left at the homes of some of the murder victims. The fact that Ms. Banks was close friends with one of the murder victims made the entire situation all the more daunting. Something told the officer that this young lady's absence must be investigated immediately and taken very seriously.

Officer Evans responded,

"The best thing for you to do is go back to Ms. Bank's home. Wait there for her. She may end up returning and if she does, we will want to be aware of that immediately. In the meantime, I will put out an all points bulletin. We will get our people to look high and low for her. We will scour the town and the surrounding areas. I will need her cell phone. An officer will come by and pick up her phone within the hour."

Peter thanked the kind officer and did as he was instructed. He prayed the entire drive home that by some miracle Tinsley would be waiting at the townhouse for him.

He entered the home and was struck by the vast, empty feel of it. Gloom and dread weighed him down into the ground. His heart raced at an alarming speed. The room started to spin and his muscles tensed and trembled. Peter sunk to the floor and began to cry. Wails and screams escaped him. He was aware that he was having a panic attack. His lungs felt as if they were not receiving enough oxygen. Peter's tears flowed steadily as he cradled his face into his sweaty palms.

The heartbroken man continued to sob until a firm knock sounded   at the door. He sprang up in such a haste, that the dizziness returned.

"Tinsley, is that you?" His voice begged hopefully.

Peter swung the door open and was forlorn to see that it was not Tinsley. It was a police officer. The officer gave him some encouraging words, took Tinsley's cell phone into his possession and departed again.

At least, law enforcement is looking for her. We are bound to find her. I won't give up until we locate her. In the meantime, the best thing I can do is wait here and pray for her to return.

Peter's self soothing worked enough that he was able to stabilize his breathing, stay off of the floor, sit on the sofa and pray.

37

The jet for Zurich took off right on time from the airport. Cosette slumped onto Luke's shoulder soon after they reached a cruising altitude. She had barely slept last night. Luke saw her still preparing for her interview with Ms. Winters at 3:00a.m. They left for the airport just a few hours later. He admired her dedication and passion for her new career. She was putting all of her effort into trying to solve the current serial killer case. Luke knew that a lot of her passion for this case stemmed from the fact that she, herself, had been apprehended by a serial killer. It was a miracle that his beloved fiancee was found on time and not physically harmed by the monster. Luke's pulse quickened and his face flushed with anger. Just the mere thought of how close Cosette had come to being slain was enough to make him feel crazy.

He understood that the primary purpose of their trip to Switzerland was for Cosette to interview the ailing mother of August Winters. Yet, she had barely taken a moment of free time since her police academy graduation.

After Cosette's interview, he was determined to show her the little town in his beloved country. The majority of his relatives resided in the quaint, wine village. Only his parents and Wyatt; his cousin, lived in the United States. Some of his most cherished childhood memories included summers in his town, Pachien. He would run through the vineyards and hike in the alps. He played soccer with his cousins and local friends at the school's soccer field. Every day, he would visit his grandmother for lunch. In Switzerland, lunch was generally the biggest meal of the day. When he entered his grandmother's kitchen, the dining table would be covered with delectable food. He remembered feasting on pork chops, raclette and platters of cold cuts and cheese. Luke never left his darling grandmother's house without a full belly and a satisfied heart. He could hardly wait to see her again. With pleasant thoughts dancing in his mind, Luke drifted off to sleep as well.

The jet touched down in Zurich and the couple proceeded to the car rental agency. Despite, Cosette's hearty nap during the flight, fatigue tugged at her weary eyes. Luke drove her to the hospital. She gave him a quick kiss and assembled her lap top and purse.

Cosette entered the stark white, spotless hospital. The signs were all written in German but, fortunately, Frank had already briefed her on Ms. Winters' room number. She knew exactly where she needed to go without having to ask for further directions.

Taking the elevator up, she exited on the 5th floor where the oncology unit was located. Spotting the room number, Cosette entered and was instantly face to face with Ms. Winters. She was a frail, pained looking lady. The outline of her body under the blankets appeared skeletal. The detective's heart broke for her. She could not stand to see any person or animal suffer. As a child, her father always affectionately called her "Tender Heart". She was well known to go above and beyond to help others. Throughout her life, she would bring deli foods from grocery stores or restaurant meals to homeless people. She had always wanted to have a magic wand and instantly make all of the world's suffering vanish. Since that was impossible, she at least helped out in small ways on a regular basis. Cosette plastered on a warm smile in hopes of making the dying woman more at ease.

"Ms. Winters? My name is Cosette DuPont. I am a detective from the Reno Police Department, homicide division. It is a pleasure to meet you. I understand that there was something you wanted to discuss with a member of law enforcement in regards to the recent slayings in our area? Before we start, may I get you anything? Perhaps, some water or another blanket?"

"You are very kind. I am fine. Thank you. The nurse just brought me a drink before you arrived. I can't tell you how happy I am that you are here. I assume you are aware that I am terminally ill. My days are numbered."

Cosette's heart ached at Ms. Winters' statement. She nodded and the lady continued.

"I went back and forth for months about coming forward and telling anyone what I am about to tell you. Listen, I love my kids. I almost died with this secret because of the love I have for my son, August. Then I started thinking that if my daughter was killed and someone with knowledge about who the killer is could have prevented it, I would be devastated. I decided that I needed to pass away with a clear conscious. I knew I needed to do the right thing."

Cosette was sitting at the edge of her seat, not sure what the ailing mother might say next. After receiving permission from Ms. Winters to record their interview, the meeting proceeded.

"I know that a slew of young ladies have been killed in the Tahoe area. As soon as I found out that two of the women were exes of my son, I had no doubt left that my son, is indeed, this "Water Bearer" serial killer."

Ms. Winters began to weep. Tears streamed down her gaunt face. Cosette gently and reassuringly squeezed her hand. The interview proceeded.

"My son has always had a dark side to him. I don't know why. I feel that we have given him a loving and healthy family environment. For whatever reason, he was a big troublemaker until about the age of eight and then he graduated to even more extreme activities. He has an identical twin, Alex. He is the kindest boy you'll ever meet. He is the polar opposite of August. Anyway, my poor Alex was tormented by August throughout their entire childhood. We had to bring him to the emergency room at least a half dozen times because August had been too rough with him. When Roseanne and Caprice broke up with August, he was infuriated and his ego was wounded. He would call me and tell me that they would live to regret their actions. The anger I heard in his voice was bone chilling. I suspected, already then, that he would seek revenge."

Cosette needed to find out if August had any sort of connection to the Aquarius zodiac sign or to stingray skin wallets without giving away confidential information. The detective could not risk jeopardizing the case. Yet, she did not travel all this way to not dig deeper and find out everything there was to possibly know about the sketchy August Winters.

Once Ms Winters had finished talking, Cosette proceeded carefully.

"Ms. Winters, may I ask when your son's birthday is?"

The dying lady seemed perplexed but answered dutifully,

"My twins are born on February 16th."

Cosette was hardly an expert on astrology, but she knew enough to figure out that a birthdate of February 16th did, in fact, fall under the Aquarius zodiac sign.

The detective presented Ms. Winters with a stingray skinned wallet and implored,

"Have you ever seen a wallet such as this one?"

The woman looked confused, took it into her hands and inspected it more closely.

"I have never seen a wallet like this in my life."

38

Law enforcement patrolled the streets of South Lake Tahoe and all of the surrounding towns. Tinsley was nowhere to be seen. Beaches, alleys, casinos, malls and trails were searched to no avail.

Peter waited at his girlfriend's residence. He was reaching the point of being inconsolable.

Officer Evans was tirelessly searching through Tinsley's phone. He monitored all of her text messages, safari searches, emails and social media activity. He determined that, not surprisingly, Tinsley was a very popular lady with the men. She had received countless direct messages from men on both her Facebook and

Instagram accounts. He noticed that she had been extremely flirty with her admirers a few months ago. Her flirtatious banter came to a grinding halt as soon as her romantic relationship with Peter had resumed.

The officer had been briefed on the timeline of her relationship with Peter. She definitely showed interest in these men in the past, but it was clear to Officer Evans that she was fully committed to Peter now. Nothing on her cell phone seemed suspicious. None of the messages she had received gave a stalker feel to them. Nonetheless, he needed to research every single gentleman who had reached out to her. That was standard protocol. He always took every case seriously, but seeing the hurt in Mr. Novak's eyes only made him all the more determined to find this missing lady.

After the interview, Cosette and Luke checked into the Novotel Zurich Airport Hotel. The couple folded onto the king sized bed. To say that they were exhausted, would be a big understatement. Cosette was generally religious about removing her make up and adhering to her stringent skin care routine prior to bedtime. Tonight was an exception. Cosette was so fatigued that she essentially collapsed onto the bed, with a face full of makeup, before she fell into a deep slumber.

The morning light filtered through their windows. Cosette squinted. It took her a moment to realize that she was in, none other than, the stunning country of Switzerland. She glanced over at her still sleeping, fiancé. Today was the day that they would travel to see his relatives. She was beyond excited.

Luke began to stir. They cuddled for a while. Cosette loved when he pulled her close to his chest.

They freshened up and got dressed. Then, they went to a restaurant on the lobby level of the hotel. Although the predominant language was German, Cosette was impressed about how many of the locals spoke English perfectly. The breakfast in Switzerland was entirely different from what Cosette was used to in the United States. Luke had briefed her that lunch was the most substantial meal of the day for the Swiss.

Their breakfast was hardly anything to complain about, however.

The inviting banquet was littered with freshly baked croissants, organic butter, locally sourced jams, honey, and in season fruits. The coffee was incredible. For Cosette, it had more the feel of a dessert rather than a simple cup of coffee. She was in heaven and understood Luke's obsession with the country of Switzerland.

After breakfast, they checked out of the hotel and embarked on the three hour journey to Luke's hometown, Pachien. They passed a series of charming towns. Cosette noticed that the churches were almost always located at the center of each village. Lake Geneva was awe inspiring. She had researched the famous, Chateau de Chillion. The duo drove right past the enchanting fortress. She had read that it was one of the best preserved medieval castles in Europe. It was situated on the eastern side of the lake and it was nestled directly between the picturesque towns of Montreux and Vileneuve. Cosette snapped photos from her IPhone. Spencer and her mother would not believe the beauty of this country if they did not see it for themselves.

The drive from the Zurich International Airport to Luke's hometown was incredibly scenic. At one point, they needed to go onto the Loetschenberg Car Train. It was a train which transported cars from Bern-Loetschenberg, the Switzerland midlands, to the Canton of Valais. Cosette learned that cantons in Switzerland are equivalent to states in the United States of America. The couple drove their rental car up onto the train. The excursion lasted approximately fifteen minutes. For the majority of the ride, they were enveloped in darkness. Since they were encased in a long tunnel, it was a perfect opportunity to rest their weary eyes. At the end of the journey, they arrived in the town of Goppenstein.

Cosette could sense Luke's excitement. He had been waiting to introduce her to his relatives and to his beloved town ever since they fell in love.

Cosette was in awe as they approached Pachien. The hillsides were covered with thousands of vineyards. The town was known for their exceptional wine. The area was often referred to as "Sun City" due to the higher than average amount of sunshine they received. Pachien was dotted with wineries. In fact, one of the most prominent ones belonged to Luke's aunt and uncle. His relatives had won countless awards, throughout the world for their top notch wines. She was eager to sample some.

Luke pulled into a driveway of an impressive looking Swiss chalet. A large balcony jutted out from the second story. The window sills were bursting with geraniums of the most vivid colors of apricot, lilac and a variety of reds. The roof of the home sloped gently downward with wide, overhanging eaves. Luke took Cosette's hand and guided her through an iron gate. They passed a cherry tree and a lush lawn.

The couple went up a series of marble steps and then he knocked on the front door. An utterly charming elderly lady opened the door. She reminded Cosette of a grandmother whom advertisers would use in cookie or hot chocolate commercials. She was small in stature and had exquisite, delicate features, a true living doll.

Cosette had discovered that in Switzerland it was customary to kiss three times on alternating cheeks as a greeting. They generally did not hug, which was more usual in the United States. Luke's grandmother, Emma, ushered them into the kitchen. Her warmth and enthusiasm was infectious. Every burner on the stove top was in use. Pots were boiling and pans were sizzling. His hospitable grandmother had been cooking up a storm in preparation for their arrival.

A tall, strongly built gentleman with handsome features, entered the room. He was Luke's grandfather, Oliver. His icy blue eyes shined and it was evident that he was overcome with happiness to be reunited with his grandson.

Throughout the lunch, a parade of relatives came to join them. Uncles, aunts and cousins were seated snuggly around the beautifully decorated dining table. The room was filled with laughter and love.

As the meal was coming to a close, Luke's delightful and kind hearted, Uncle Leonard, handed Cosette a gift. She was touched by the unexpected gesture. The entire family watched as she unwrapped the goody. She gasped when she saw the contents of the box. It was a modern, supremely elegant, black and gold, Rado watch. Never having owned a Swiss watch and moved by the generous uncle's kindness, Cosette's soul became flooded with sunshine. Uncle Leonard's sparkling, ocean blue eyes and broad smile illuminated the room. Cosette could certainly understand why Luke was so attached to his uncle.

To top the day off, Luke's charming Aunt Lena gave the duo a deluxe tour of their winery. It was located directly next door to the grandparent's house. Cosette was blown away by the intricate wood carvings, state of the art wine making equipment, and the architecture of the building. She was intrigued by all of the large, wooden barrels the wine was stored in.

Next, Luke's Uncle Louis gave them a walking tour of the sun drenched rows of vines. The distinguished gentleman was an expert on both the business side of the winery and also the actual wine making component. He was a fascinating man. The vines extended as far as the eye could see. They topped the afternoon off with wine tasting in a private room within the winery.

After they bid the relatives goodbye, Luke said,

"Cosette, I want to bring you to a place which is very special to me. Are you up for a ten minute walk?"

"You bet I am!"

The couple meandered up a hillside. Stations of the cross were featured along the path. The majority of the 1500 residents of Pachien were devout Catholics. As a visitor, their devotion became quickly apparent. The church was the center of the idyllic village. Many of the homes displayed crosses at the front or the interior of their homes.

The sky was powder blue in color. Only a few lingering clouds remained. The path ahead shimmered in the heat of the afternoon sun. The chalets were bathed in a warm, golden light. At last, they reached the top of the hill. What Cosette saw, took her breath away. A lonely chapel stood proudly at the summit. Its only companion was a fountain display and a wooden bench which was positioned perfectly for its guests to look over the breathtaking town below. A large cross was perched front and center near the edge of the cliff. Vineyards encircled the hilltop. Luke guided Cosette over to the bench. They stared silently at the intense beauty of his homeland. A soft, warm breeze caressed their faces. Luke began to explain why this chapel was so special to him.

"As you know, I spent most of my summers here in my childhood. My time in Pachien was magical and unforgettable. But, let's face it, everyone has off days, no matter how optimistic and happy they are naturally wired to be. The handful of times I felt gloomy, I would walk up here, go into the chapel and pray. After, I would sit on this very bench and gaze out at my village. By doing this, my worries faded right before my eyes. It worked every single time. This will always be my place, my heart, my soul. I have a little surprise for you, Cosette."

Luke pulled out a red, velvet jewelry box.

"Please open it. I ordered this gift before I knew we were going to visit Switzerland. It was supposed to be your birthday present. Little did I know that I would have the opportunity to give the gift to you at the actual site."

Cosette's interest was piqued. She opened the box and spotted a beautiful necklace. The pendant featured a photo of the chapel. On the back of the pendant stood the coordinates of the chapel in Pachien. Cosette gasped. It was the most thoughtful gift she had ever received.

"I am speechless and that sure doesn't happen very often. I will never take this necklace off. It means more to me than I can possibly tell you."

A single tear cascaded down Cosette's cheek. Luke pulled her close to him.

Pachien was the most magical village she had ever been to. It would be a day she would never forget.

39

Sutter Munro scheduled an emergency staff meeting for that morning. Law enforcement officers and detectives filed into the conference room. The air conditioning was working overtime. The air felt frigid and the room smelled of an interesting mix of deodorant and coffee beans. They all knew that whenever an emergency meeting was called, it was almost never good news. The chief called for silence and began to speak.

"I know you are all aware that Tinsley Banks has been missing since yesterday. In my opinion, all signs point to that she is the latest victim of the "Water Bearer". We have scoured this town and the surrounding areas. She has disappeared. There has not been any activity on her credit cards or on her bank account. Tinsley was known at the casino as being a very accountable and loyal employee. She never even arrived late for her shifts a single time. Whenever a person disappears, of course, we must consider that suicide is a possibility. Based on the investigation, I have determined that this option is highly unlikely. For one thing, she disappeared without her car. She would not have gotten very far on foot. We would have found her. Also, she was in what seems to be a happy and healthy romantic relationship. Her texts and emails lead me to conclude that she was in a positive mental state. In fact, she had even been researching local wedding venues. A lady who is that in love and excited about the future would rarely think of ending her life. August Winters has continued to be at the top of our person of interest list. Cosette DuPont just interviewed his mother in Zurich, Switzerland. She sent me the audio of their interview. Unfortunately, the mom did not give us any information which we could use to apprehend August. His zodiac sign is

Aquarius but that is hardly grounds to arrest someone. You figure that approximately one in every twelve people on the planet fall into the same category. Ms. Winters seemed clueless when Cosette showed her one of the stingray skin wallets. That doesn't work in our favor either. Yet, she believes her son is our killer. We can't close a case because of someone's belief. We need much more concrete evidence. Let's continue to fan out and search for Ms. Banks. Knock on her neighbors' doors. Interview her coworkers and friends. Maybe somebody saw something which could give us some information on her whereabouts. If we don't find her quickly, it will be too late. Unfortunately, my guess is that she has already been slain."

Peter continued to wait breathlessly at Tinsley's townhome. He had not been able to sleep since his girlfriend had gone missing. He was inconsolable. Staring at the front door, while holding Putscho on his lap, the minutes turned into hours. He held the fluffy orange feline closely and wept into his luxurious fur. This was the closest Peter had ever come to losing his mind. He was generally an easy going, happy go lucky, type of person. Without Tinsley, his upbeat mood all came to a grinding halt.

He loved her and needed her. There was no doubt that the heartbroken young man would not survive losing her again. He kept staring at Tinsley's social media friend list. Something was telling him that the answer of where his love was could potentially get answered by looking at her contacts. He adored everything about her but he also knew that she had a tendency to be an overly trusting person. Tinsley was outgoing. Her extreme beauty might have been intimidating to others, but her warmth and humor made up for that. She remained approachable due to her friendliness despite her good looks. Had she inadvertently corresponded with a killer?

Tommy and James had become fast friends. They went on every assignment together. This morning the duo was working undercover at the Crystal Waters Casino. Dressed in jeans and t-shirts, they blended in perfectly amongst the other casino guests. Tommy positioned himself at a slot machine while James played at the Blackjack table. Both of them were seated in the area where Roseanne and Tinsley had worked. Ordering tonic waters, each of the detectives had perfect vantage points of the employees and fellow guests. Melissa was training two newly hired cocktail waitresses, Brenda and Penelope. Melissa looked worn out and stressed. The new hires appeared tense and harried. The guests were demanding and impatient.

A rough looking man with frizzy white hair and a sleeve tattoo was seated at the slot machine next to Tommy. He was becoming belligerent with Melissa. After delivering his sixth shot, Melissa informed him that she was not going to serve him any more alcohol. He snapped and shouted,

"This would never have happened with Tinsley. She always treated me like a king. I miss her. Why can't you be more like her?"

Melissa's face reddened and she retorted,

"Well, I don't want to be more like her. Tinsley didn't know how to set boundaries. I am not surprised she ended up getting killed!"

Tommy kept his composure and continued to sip on his drink.

I can't believe what I just heard. Everything about Melissa's words are suspicious. First, she's clearly jealous of Tinsley. Second, Tinsley is listed as missing. Her whereabouts remain unknown. Why would Melissa state so confidently that she was murdered?

Melissa circled back around to Tommy a few minutes later.

"Can I get you another drink, hon?"

"I would love one more. You ladies seem slammed today. Are you short staffed?"

"We sure are. It has been a zoo around here."

"Is the casino looking to hire some more cocktail waitresses to lighten your load?"

"Yes, thank goodness. The sooner we get more help, the better off we will be. We are booked solid every day of the week because of conventions. The shifts have been awful."

Tommy paused for a moment and then stated, "I think I know the perfect candidate. She has been looking for a job."

"Great! Here, take this business card. It's the manager's contact information. She can schedule an interview through him."

40

Cosette and Luke had just landed at the Reno International Airport when Frank called Cosette's cell phone.

"Welcome home, Cosette. I hate to bother you as soon as you get back into town but Tommy and James have been monitoring the Crystal Waters Casino and they feel pretty sure we may find a lot of answers to our serial killer case there. It so happens, they are currently hiring more cocktail waitresses. I was wondering if you would be game to apply for the job and work there undercover? A lot of times, people on the inside get a lot more information than law enforcement would. As a coworker, you will probably befriend them. They will trust you and that is when secrets start getting spilled."

"That sounds like a great opportunity for us to get more inside information," agreed Cosette. "I will call as soon as I get home and try to schedule an interview as quickly as possible."

Rubbing her eyes, she felt an overwhelming fatigue. The jet lag was hitting her hard. Luke and Cosette returned home and received a warm and excited welcome from Spencer, Cosette's mother and the pets. The duo had only be away for a few days but they had already missed their family a great deal.

After sitting down for some coffee and catching up, Cosette knew it was time to get back to business. There would be plenty of time to sleep this evening. While reminding herself to use her pseudonym, she dialed the number Frank had given her. A cheerful voice picked up after the first ring.

"Tyson Gilman, here, how may I help you?"

"Hello, Mr. Gilman. This is Jenna Donovan. I am calling to inquire about the cocktail waitress position. Are you still hiring?"

"We sure are. I am conducting interviews all this week. Crystal Waters has a few openings currently. Do you have any experience waitressing and are you twenty-one years of age or older?"

"I am well over twenty-one years old and I have two years of waitressing experience. I just relocated from Roseville."

"Terrific, would you be able to come by for an interview tomorrow morning at 10:00 am?"

"Yes, that works very well."

"I will mark you down. Just come to the cocktail lounge area and ask for me. Oh, and please bring your resume."

After bidding each other goodbye, Cosette called Frank to give him an update. He was pleased that she had already scheduled an interview.

"So, here is the thing, Cosette. As I am sure you have already figured out, you recently met a few of the Crystal Waters Casino employees at a bar. It is crucial that you continue using the name Jenna. It is standard procedure for potential employers to run background checks. I will ask Sutter to assign one of his tech experts to get your resume and background information aligned. We will make sure you receive the resume before today is over. That way it will give you some time to memorize the details of the document. Any questions?"

"No, I think I am clear on what I am supposed to do. If I think of anything, I will let you know. Thanks so much, Frank. I will swing by the office later this evening to pick up the resume. See you soon."

The day went by in a blur. Finally, evening arrived. Cosette had picked up her documents and was sitting at her office desk, memorizing details about her fabricated life. In her pseudo life, she was twenty-seven years old and had worked as a waitress at a restaurant named, The Hungry Hog, in Roseville. Conveniently, it was impossible for the manager, Tyson, to receive a referral about her since the restaurant had recently gone out of business. Sutter's technical expert had covered all bases.

Feeling well rehearsed and confident for her interview tomorrow, Cosette drifted into a well deserved and deep slumber.

41

Melissa had been hooking up with him for months and he had insisted that she keep their affair a secret. She ventured over to his place at least once a week. She knew he was the infamous serial killer since he had inadvertently admitted it to her one night after heavy drinking. Melissa became even more enthralled with him after becoming privy to his killing tendencies. She loved bad boys. She always had. This man was broken and deranged. It intoxicated her.

Despite feeling fatigued after her grueling shift, Melissa darted to his place. She couldn't stay away and she was aware that she was completely obsessed with him. Swinging by a convenience store along her route, Melissa picked up a bottle of Jack Daniels and Coke.

He is going to love my little surprise. I have been counting the seconds to see him all day. I know he couldn't care less about me but at least I am getting a part of him for now. Who knows? Maybe in time he will end up falling hopelessly in love with him. I want, no I need, to spend the rest of my life with him.

Refreshing her eye shadow and lipstick, combing her frizzy locks, she pulled herself out of the car and knocked on his door. Her broody lover swung the door open with a scowl.

"What are you doing here? I wasn't expecting you!"

Melissa was taken aback by his cold demeanor.

"Sweetheart, don't you remember that I texted you before my shift and told you that I would come over tonight?" she inquired hopefully.

He was clearly inebriated and in a very foul mood.

"Not really. What do you have there? Jack Daniels? I guess you can come in. I need another drink!"

Masking her emotional pain from his hurtful comments, Melissa forced a smile on her face and responded, "Great, my love. I have been dying to see you all day."

Her love interest grunted as if her words disgusted him.

The brutish man pounded back one stiff drink after the next. Melissa fought back tears and thought,

I *should be used to this by now. He has never treated me well. Why does this man make me lose all my common sense? He makes me crazy with love and desire. I feel like a school girl around him.*

The rest of the night continued as all of their time together did. They drank until they both could no longer see straight. Then the duo went back to his bedroom and were intimate. Her lover was mechanical, expressionless and cold. As usual, he refused to kiss her. Melissa fought back tears. When their interlude was over, he told her to get out. She did the walk of shame back to her awaiting vehicle. Melissa cried the entire way home.

Cosette arrived at the Crystal Waters Casino ahead of schedule. She reviewed her notes one last time and ensured that she had all of the appropriate identification.

A pleasant looking gentleman with round, soft, maple colored eyes and chiseled, high cheekbones approached her.

"You must be Jenna Donovan?"

"I sure am. Are you Mr. Gilman?"

"Yes, but please call me Tyson. It is a pleasure to meet you, Jenna. Why don't we head back to my office and we can start the interview?"

The interview went off without a hitch. Tyson was taken by Cosette's professionalism and polished responses. She was hired on the spot.

"Would it be possible for you to start tomorrow? Our afternoon shift is short staffed."

"That works perfectly for me."

"Terrific, just what I wanted to hear. Melissa is our head cocktail waitress. She will train you. I think you will enjoy working with her. As you probably are aware, one of our employees was tragically murdered. Another employee is missing. We have been dealing with a lot of heartache lately. Melissa was close friends with both ladies. She has had a particularly difficult time. Nonetheless, she is an outstanding server and I have no doubt that you two will get along perfectly. Now, as far as your uniform, please go to the mezzanine level and see Donna Spinel. She will fit you for your uniform and then you will be all set to begin tomorrow."

"Thank you! I am very excited to start. I will head over to Ms. Spinel now. What time shall I report tomorrow?"

"Tomorrow's shift is from 1:00 p.m. until 9:00 p.m.

Welcome aboard!"

42

Cosette donned her work uniform and frowned as she glanced in the mirror. The skirt barely managed to cover her behind. Her strappy, silver heels felt as high as the Eiffel Tower. Her feet already ached and she hadn't even left the house yet.

It will be all worth it, if my undercover work helps us catch the killer. We can't let another innocent life be taken.

With that affirmative thought, Cosette headed to the casino. Melissa greeted her warmly as she reported to the station.

"Jenna? Hey, I know you! We met at El's Hideout after the bike-a-thon not too long ago. It is great to see you. If I remember correctly, you were living in Roseville at the time? What a fluke that we now get to work together. I love it!"

"Wow! You have a great memory. That is true. I decided I needed a change of pace. Tahoe is gorgeous. I figured I would live here for a while and see how I like it. So far, it is great. I am excited to be working here."

"Well, just follow me. I bet you will get the hang of the job in no time. We go out to the customers and ask them what they would like to drink. Then we march over to the bartender and he will fill our orders. After that, we deliver the drinks. It is as simple as that. Let me introduce you to our bartender, Aaron."

Cosette followed Melissa over to the bar area. A young, slimly built man with caterpillar like eyebrows and shoulder length auburn hair was furiously mixing drinks. He seemed anxious and harried.

"Aaron, I would like you to meet our newest server, Jenna. Jenna, this is Aaron McGregor. "

Cosette startled but made a point of making her surprise undetectable. She recognized his name. Aaron was the boyfriend of one of the murder victims, Faith Gunder. The last she had heard, he was an employee at the Silver Skate Rink. Why was he now working at the Crystal Waters Casino? Fortunately, she herself had never interviewed him so she was not concerned that he could recognize her. During the shift, there were a few minutes of downtime. This was Cosette's chance to do some investigating.

"Melissa, I have been meaning to tell you how sorry I am that your coworker, Tinsley, is missing. I can only imagine how heartbreaking that is, especially after already losing Roseanne."

"Yeah, it has been awful. I am depressed and scared. I feel like I constantly need to look over my shoulder. Lots of people have suffered because of this killer. In fact, Aaron's girlfriend, Faith, was one of his victim's also. He is heartbroken."

Cosette feigned surprise by Melissa's statement.

"Oh no, I wasn't aware of that. How tragic! Did Faith work here also?"

"No, she worked at the Silver Skate. She was killed in their parking lot after she locked the place up for the night."

Just then, Aaron walked over to Cosette and Melissa.

"Hey, what are you two chatting about?"

Cosette knew this was her opportunity to mention his girlfriend's demise and gauge his reaction.

"Melissa was just telling me about your girlfriend's passing. I am so sorry. How have you been doing?"

Aaron's entire demeanor shifted and he scowled.

"I don't want to talk about it!"

He stormed off towards the bar area.

Melissa chimed, "Don't take it personally. He gets very moody whenever Faith is mentioned."

"Maybe I shouldn't have brought up such a sensitive subject. Melissa, what's the word around here? Are there any theories about who the killer is?"

"Boy, you sure ask a lot of questions. No, nobody has any clue who the killer is. One popular theory is that it is connected to gang activity."

"I wasn't aware that there are gangs in Lake Tahoe?" pressed Cosette.

"There isn't really but they come here from larger cities like Reno and Carson City."

Gabe, the handsome pool attendant interrupted their conversation. Cosette recognized him from the evening she was at the bar. He appeared surprised when he saw Cosette.

"Hey, I know you. We met at the bar not too long ago. Could you tell me your name again?"

"Yes, I remember you. I'm Jenna."

"I'm Gabe. You are working here now?"

"Exactly, I just moved to the area. I am loving it so far."

"Awesome, welcome aboard! My shift just ended. It was crazy busy at the pool today. I need a drink. Could one of you beautiful ladies get me a Long Island Iced Tea?"

Gabe meandered over to a small booth in the cocktail lounge.

Once he was out of ear shot, Cosette prodded, "Wow, he is a very good looking man. He must be a nice distraction during shifts."

"I guess. I'll go get Gabe his drink."

The Arctic Tundra was warmer than how Melissa was suddenly behaving towards Cosette. Ever since she had questioned her about the murders, the mysterious cocktail waitress, had started to freeze her out and give clipped responses.

Cosette was only a couple hours into her first shift and it was clearly evident to her, that the casino would prove to be a gold mine of information for their murder investigation.

43

Tommy and James were parked on a tree lined, heavily shaded, side road. They were staking out Lindsey and Hank Plantine's house. Cosette had updated them that the husband, Hank, had admitted to having a months long affair with one of the murder victims, Patsy Goodwin. Both gentlemen were aware that over half of all murdered women were killed by a current or former romantic partner and being involved in an affair increased the likelihood of violence. Those facts made Hank a person of interest.

Stakeouts had a tendency to be tedious but Tommy and James made the best of their time together. Although they needed to concentrate and observe, they still were able to do coin rolls across their knuckles. They had mini competitions throughout their shifts. Tommy was especially skilled at it. He would place a quarter between his thumb and index finger and used the thumb to push the coin across the back of his finger. Then he would masterfully raise his middle finger and use it to push one side of the coin down. By doing this, the coin then flipped onto the back of his middle finger.

"There's got to be some kind of local competitions we could enter for this," Tommy stated enthusiastically.

"If this were an Olympic sport, you'd get the gold. You've gotten darn good." James complimented his partner sincerely.

Just then, the gentlemen noticed a movement from the direction of the Plantine's front door. The detectives were positioned in a way which made them inconspicuous but they still managed to have an optimal vantage point of the home. It was the ideal stakeout position.

Hank hastily exited the home, locked the heavy, wooden front door and made a bee-line to the car parked on the driveway.

"It's go time," whispered Tommy.

Hank's jeep made a sharp, right′ turn onto the road, and off he went. Stalling for a few moments, James and Tommy followed suit. They were in for a long ride. Hank proceeded to drive towards Reno. He exited the freeway into the town of Sparks and pulled into a newly paved parking lot of a well known brothel. The building consisted of three stories and the paint colors reminded Tommy of a birthday cake. The brothel was entirely pink with white trim.

"Well, I'll be darn!" exclaimed Tommy. This doesn't tie Hank to the murders but he is definitely a dog. Some marriage they have. Looks like the affair with Patsy was not his only indiscretion."

James agreed, "It is sad. He seems rudderless to me but I am just not convinced he is our killer. Call it a gut instinct, if you will."

"I am kind of getting the same feeling," chimed Tommy. "But my intuition has not always been 100% accurate. I say we continue to keep an eye on him. Who knows, maybe he will get drunk and sloppy and spill   all his deepest secrets to someone in the brothel. Let's hang out for a while. Once he leaves, we can go inside and see if anyone is willing to talk to us."

44

Melissa could barely wait to finish her shift and go to her lover's home.

This new waitress, Jenna, is grating on my last nerve. She is asking too many questions about the murders for my comfort. She is a busy body. I am going to need to tell him that she is poking her nose around where it doesn't belong.

Melissa dashed to his home after her shift was over. Before knocking on his door, she touched up her lipstick, combed her unruly hair and took a breath mint. As usual, he greeted her with minimal enthusiasm. He seemed chronically annoyed by her.

His attitude is starting to get old. I do everything for him and all I get is this awful treatment. Is he forgetting that I know he is the killer? He sure is confident that I will keep my mouth shut. I am going to need more of a commitment from him if I am going to continue to keep his secret.

Despite his grouchy greeting, she forced on her mega watt smile and cooed,

"Well, hello lover boy. I missed you all day."

"Uh huh, whatever," he responded in a frosty tone.

"Well, is that any way to greet your love?"

"Melissa, if I had a dime for every time I told you that I don't have any feelings for you. Zip! Hooking up on occasion is fine but we will never be more than that. Get that through your thick head already. Do I need to put it into sky writing for you to finally get it?"

Even though Melissa had heard these words from him countless times, it still stung her to hear them. He acted like she was useless and that her feelings were irrelevant. Tonight, she had a plan. It was time to progress their relationship.

After plying him with liquor, she enticed him into the bedroom. Roper, his snake, always gave her the creeps. He seemed to stare into her with soulless eyes.

"Sweetie pie, I have been meaning to talk to you about something."

"Ugh, what now?"

"Well, I have been very loyal to you. After all, I know ALL of your secrets."

"What is that supposed to mean? You sure as hell had better not be threatening me!"

"No, sweetheart, of course not. I just feel that it is time to take our relationship to the next level."

"We don't, have a relationship, Melissa. I won't repeat that to you again."

Melissa could feel her temper rising. Her patience was wearing thin.

"Ok, I think I am not being clear enough. I want more from you than I am getting. I refuse to just be some casual hook-up for you. You told me everything you have done and I still love you, warts and all. I will keep your secrets forever, *if,* we are in a committed relationship."

A wave of violent fury rose within him. His jaw clenched and his muscles began to twitch. Ever since he was a young boy, his eyes would furiously blink if he was angry. His eyes were now opening and closing at a lightning quick pace. He could feel the demon rising within him.

How dare this worthless, waste of space has the nerve to threaten me. I can't believe I even let her live as long as she has. I was wasted out of my mind when I stupidly told her about my favorite pastime. This woman needs to get eliminated now. I sure as hell won't take a fall because of Melissa.

His pulse was racing faster than the speed of a fighter jet. He bared his teeth at her like a rabid wolf. Sweat poured down his strained features.

Melissa saw a demonic expression cross his face. Her eyes widened and her shoulders slumped. She sat on her hands to prevent them from trembling.

What was I thinking to threaten him. I love him and I was sure he would never hurt me.

From the callous look he was giving her, Melissa knew that she was about to die. Goose bumps littered her arms. Her breathing became raspy. Her fight or flight reflex kicked in. She attempted to dodge out of his grasp but it was too late. His strong hands encircled her neck and she started to struggle to breathe. Melissa had always heard that a dying person's life flashes through her mind during the final moments. This is exactly what happened to her. She saw her mother pushing her on a swing at the Golden Gate Park in San Francisco when she was five years old. Then she saw her Junior Prom, first day of work at an ice cream parlor as a teen, her first kiss ever, a sleepover with her childhood best friend…then darkness. The life drained from her body. Melissa went limp.

Hank exited the brothel two hours later. He looked satisfied and spent. Tommy and James watched the man drive away. Once the detectives were certain that he had indeed left the area, they proceeded into the establishment.

The smoke in the air overwhelmed their senses. Tommy gagged momentarily. He had been a chain smoker, himself, about a decade ago. It took all of his strength, but he was finally able to kick the habit. Now, the scent of cigarette smoke made him feel nauseous. He pushed through the queasiness and proceeded over to the bar area. One of the tallest women he had every encountered greeted him. She had white-blond, stick straight hair, black, impenetrable eyes and sleeve tattoos depicting dragons and unicorns on both arms. Her name tag stated, "Delores". She welcomed Tommy and James with a booming, almost gruff voice.

"What can I get for you gentlemen tonight? You strike me as the Gin and tonic types?"

James responded,

Two mineral waters will do. Thank you."

"What? Are you in some sort of Alcoholics Anonymous program?" Sandy prodded. As a bartender, it isn't every day that I get orders for nonalcoholic drinks here."

"No, that isn't the case," responded Tommy. "We just aren't in the mood for cocktails tonight."

"Suit yourself."

As Delores handed them their drinks, Tommy pulled out a photo of Hank Plantine and showed it to the bartender.

"Does this gentleman look familiar to you?" enquired the detective.

"He sure does. He was here today. He left not too long ago. Why do you ask?"

Tommy had to proceed with caution. He was aware that she could legally refuse to answer his questions at any moment.

James responded, "We are concerned friends. We just want to make sure he is ok."

Dolores hesitated. The silence between them was awkward. She placed her flaming red, coffin shaped fingernails along her chin and appeared to be contemplating her next response.

"He seemed pretty happy to me. He visits Brenda regularly."

"Is Brenda available to speak with for a minute?" continued Tommy hopefully.

"Yeah, she's around here somewhere. Brenda is a petite redhead. Today, she's wearing a black, polka dot tank top and a short, jean skirt. You can probably find her in the ping pong table area."

The detectives thanked Delores and proceeded to the area where the ping pong tables were. Tommy and James spotted Brenda immediately. She was dancing on one of the tables while belting out the song, "Oops, I did it again" by Brittany Spears. Tommy thought that her voice was quite impressive. They watched her continue singing her melody. When the song was over, she sprang off of the table in one graceful movement and sat at the nearby bar. This was the detectives' chance. As the duo approached her, Brenda's face lit up and she stated coyly,

"Are you two hotties looking to party?"

"We just have a couple questions for you," said James.

"My measurements are 36-24-36 and I am a Virgo." Brenda burst into a fit of laughter after her remark.

"That's interesting to know but we have some questions about one of your regular customers, Hank. In fact, he visited you this evening," continued Tommy

"Yeah, what about him?"

"Does he see you often?"

"Hmmm, I would say he comes in a couple times a month. Hank is a nice guy but he just seems very sad always."

"Why so?"

"He was really hung up on some chick who got murdered. Let me try to remember her name...Patsy Godfried."

"Do you mean Patsy Goodwin?"

"Yeah, that's it. He was super into her and she dumped him. He never saw the break up coming. Some months later that awful, local serial killer got her. Hank was destroyed. He started seeing me after her death. You see, I am also kind of a therapist to my customers," boasted Brenda.

Tommy continued,

"Did he ever mention to you if he suspected who the killer was or say anything else about the case?"

"I thought it was kind of crazy, but he actually thought his wife, Lindsey, was involved in Patsy's death. He was dumb enough to admit his feelings for Patsy to his wife. Obviously, she flipped out and not long after this incident his girlfriend was killed. He blamed himself for her death."

"Why is that?"

"Hank is convinced that had he not gotten tipsy and confessed his feelings to his wife that night, Patsy would still be alive."

Tommy and James thanked Brenda for her time and exited into the cold, desert night. They walked across the gritty sand of the parking lot shivering. The heavy silence was interrupted by the eerie baying of coyotes in the distance. As the wind howled, the dust from the ground billowed around the detectives. Tommy detected the distinct taste of copper in his mouth from the swirling particles. He wiped dirt and sweat from his brow. It had been a long day. Both of the detectives were eager to call it a night and return to their respective homes. Fatigue weighed them down. Rest was mandatory at this point.

The unapologetic, harsh shrill of Cosette's cell phone roused her out of a deep sleep.

"Hello?" Cosette murmured wearily.

"Cosette, this is Frank. I hate calling you so early but, sadly, the killer has struck again."

His words sent chills up and down her spine.

"Oh no, what happened? Who is the victim this time?"

"Brace yourself. Your co-worker, Melissa, was discovered along the West County trail about an hour ago. It was evident that she was strangled and there was an Aquarius pendant found on her corpse, along the chest area. The medical examiner is with the body now. Upon, initial inspection, I think it is safe to assume that this is the work of our serial killer. Obviously, the examiner will be able to confirm or deny this pretty soon."

Cosette was deeply saddened and shocked by Frank's words. He continued ,"Where there is smoke, there is fire. Two employees from the Crystal Waters Casino have been murdered and a third one is missing and presumed dead. These murders have got to be connected to the casino. Your job there has never been more critical. We need all eyes and ears around that place. What time is your shift today?"

"I start at 11a.m."

"Great, you will be able to see the reactions of many of the employees as they hear the news of Melissa's death. Their response is critical. Cosette, I know you are a very observant and intuitive person. Keep your eyes peeled. Trust your gut. We need to get this monster. While you are doing that, Tommy and James will interview everyone close to Melissa. I'll assign Olympia to study her social media platforms."

"Ok, Frank. Consider it done. I will keep you posted throughout the day. I know that Melissa went home with Tyler Herman after the evening we spent at the bar. It was clear that they were much more than friends. I get the feeling they weren't going back to his place to sing around the campfire. I will keep an especially close eye on his behavior and reaction."

Peter woke up with a start. His entire body was drenched in sweat. Ever since Tinsley had vanished, his nights were filled with nightmares.

Often, he even woke up screaming. His work shifts were the most difficult. He had to plaster on a fake smile and just go through the motions.

I can't go on like this much longer. I am a wreck. The guilt is beginning to destroy my spirit. What am I supposed to do? Calm down...things will get better again. I just need to pray.

Peter drifted back into a fitful sleep. A nightmare greeted him instantly. Tinsley was running towards him with outstretched arms. Just as she was about to embrace him, Peter's strong, muscular hands reached for her and strangled her. He watched the life drain out of her. Tinsley's eyes stared at him vacantly. He began to laugh hysterically as he gazed at her corpse. Peter awoke again coated in perspiration.

45

He hated having to kill her. Not because he felt even the slightest hint of remorse but rather because his murders were always calculated down to the last detail. Spur of the moment homicides were not his thing. Over the years, he had managed to read every true crime serial killer book published. He studied the killers meticulously. Emulating their strong points and avoiding their errors was essential. Based on his extensive research, he was aware that a spontaneous homicide often led to the killer getting caught. In fact, it was a recipe for disaster.

But I didn't have a choice. Melissa was a loose cannon. I should have killed her months ago when I blurted out my secret to her. I was foolish to delay the inevitable. Sure enough, not murdering her then, caught up with me now. She threatened to expose me. Nobody threatens me and gets away with it! Ever! I think I covered all of my tracks. Dragging her to that trail while it was still dark was brilliant. I couldn't have her body anywhere near my home. I am pretty confident she didn't tell anyone she was coming over to my house after work last night. After all, her best friends are dead, our affair is top secret and she surely would never confide in that pesky new hire waitress, Jenna. Yup, I think I am pretty safe. They won't trace her murder back to me.

Feeling satisfied that he covered all his tracks, he took an extra long shower and collapsed into bed.

Murder sure is vigorous exercise. I am exhausted.

The killer laughed uproariously at his thoughts, slumped into the fetal position and delved into a deep slumber.

Dr Westford had been hunched over the steel examining table for hours. Despite having years of autopsy experience under his belt, it pained him to see the severely bruised and battered victim before him.

Such a young woman. She had her whole life in front of her. If I never see another murder victim again, it will be too soon. We need to find this killer and stop him. If we don't hurry, more women will die. I have no doubt about that.

Dr. Westford's gloomy thoughts briefly stalled the examination of the victim. He took a long swig of coffee and forced himself to get back to the task at hand.

Cosette's work shift was stressful. The cocktail lounge was packed and the customers were inpatient and demanding. When she finally had a minute to rest, a wave of nausea hit her. She had been feeling queasy for a week now, chalking it up to a mild stomach bug. The smell of alcohol and coffee only exasperated her symptoms. She had noticed that when she put ice cubes or a mint in her mouth, the nausea subsided. Cosette finally had a minute to rest.

She darted to the pool center to get some ice from the ice machine.

As she entered the humid pool center, she saw one of her coworkers doing laps in the tepid water. He greeted her warmly and propped himself up on the pool's edge to talk to her.

"Hey, Jenna, how is your shift going?"

Cosette responded, "Ugh, don't even ask. We have been slammed all day. There's finally a little reprieve so I came here to get a cup of ice."

"Well, you take it easy. It's a new job for you. There's a natural learning curve, so, don't let yourself get too overwhelmed."

"I'll try. Thanks for the advice. Enjoy your swim."

The gentleman turned to restart his laps. As he did, Cosette saw something which almost knocked her over. On his right shoulder, stood a tattoo of a stingray. On his left shoulder, was a tattoo depicting the Aquarius Water Bearer. Cosette stifled a gasp. She had become all too familiar with the Aquarius zodiac sign image. Maintaining her composure, she sauntered to the ice machine, filled her cup and bid the coworker goodbye.

My God! He is the killer. I have no doubt. His tattoos are far too much of a coincidence. I only have one more hour of my shift left. I need to calm down and act like nothing is out of the ordinary. Melissa's locker is right next to mine. There must be a way I can get into it. Maybe I will find some helpful clues. I have always suspected that Tinsley was not murdered yet and that she is being held captive somewhere. With the exception of Amber Trident, all the other bodies were found fairly soon after their deaths. Plus, we don't even know for sure if Amber was one of the Water Bearer's victims. What if Tinsley is still alive? What if that monster is keeping her somewhere? She won't be alive much longer. I need to go search around his house. I will look at the schedule and see when his next shift is. I'll plan to go around his home when I know he is here.

The moment the shift ended, Cosette raced to the locker area. Luck was on her side. She was alone in the room. She had been wracking her brain about details Melissa had mentioned about her life. People often created passwords which had significance. She recalled that her deceased coworker's birthday was on October 4th, 1993.

"Hmm, the combination requires six digits. Let me try 10-1993.

Cosette inputted the numbers. The lock did not budge. After a few different combinations, she tried, 10-04-93. To her excitement, the lock sprung loose and opened. Taking a final glance around the room, she opened Melissa's locker and used the light on her cell phone to illuminate the dark interior. Cosette was surprised, but relieved, that law enforcement had not yet secured the contents of the murder victim's locker. Melissa's locker was strewn with a variety of items. Cosette found hair ties, Motrin, a bikini and even a moldy salami sandwich. As the detective neared the bottom of the locker, she spotted a notebook. Focussing her light on the item, Cosette could see that it appeared to be a diary. It was navy blue in color and the front was adorned with images of the moon and stars. Slipping the book into her bag, Cosette went into the restroom. She did not want to risk getting caught with the item.

Once locked into a stall, Cosette began leafing through the diary. At first, Melissa had written about a girl's night out, her job interview at the Crystal Waters Casino, a breast augmentation surgery she had undergone. However, soon after, the tone of the diary changed entirely. Melissa was in love. The man's name was not mentioned. She discussed spending the night with him on multiple entries.

It is official! I have fallen in love. It has been a long time since I have felt this giddy, a very long time. He is so sexy. I cant get him out of my mind. I go through withdrawal symptoms when I can't see him for even a day.

Then the tone of the diary began to change.

Oh wow, dear diary. Have I got juicy details to tell you. After a night of drinking, my man confessed that he is the local serial killer. I know most women would be mortified. Am I weird that it excites me so much? You know, I've always loved the bad boys. And I especially love him.

Cosette's heart raced. Melissa was giving a lot of information but, so far, she had not mentioned the mystery man's name. After reading several more entires, the detective hit the gold mine.

He gets so mad when I bring up that it is exciting for me that he is a killer. He tells me that I am even more deranged than he is. He can be cold to me sometimes. Actually, he is cold to me most of the time. I will get him to commit to me one day. I know I will. Eventually, we will get married. I will personalize all of our bath towels. How cute will it be to see our names, "Melissa and Gabe" on everything?

Cosette froze in place. Her heart rate accelerated. Gabe was the man she saw doing laps in the swim center just now. The same man with the tell-tale tattoos. Everything was starting to fall into place. She went to the nearest computer, inputted her employee number and within seconds she was able to see that Gabe was scheduled to work a shift starting later this evening. Time was of the essence. If Tinsley was still alive, she probably would not be among the living for much longer. Cosette needed to find her immediately.

46

After researching Gabe's address, property information and general layout of the area, Cosette sped over to his home.

I am going to take the heat for searching Gabe's property without a warrant. I might even lose my job. This young lady will die if I don't do something immediately. If we go through the appropriate channels and secure the warrants, it may be too late. I can't risk Tinsley's life. For as long as I can remember, I have always lived strictly by the rules. I can't do that any more. I need to trust my judgement on this one. It is a matter of life or death.

On her way to Gabe's home, Cosette texted Tommy.

I know who our killer is! It is Gabe Patterson. The man who works in the pool center at the casino. He is working a shift right now. I am heading over to his house to see if I can find any more evidence. If you don't hear from me within the hour, please come looking for me. His address is 375 Lake Terrace Lane.

She parallel parked one house down from Gabe's property. Exiting the car, she secured her Glock 22 and headed over to his house. The wind howled around her as the sun was beginning to set. The sky burst into flaming colors of reds and yellows. A large flock of pigeons raced to reach their nests before complete darkness arrived. The jagged mountains in the distance were covered in shade, almost as if their mother had tucked them in under a cozy blanket for the evening.

The detective surveyed the property, looking for security cameras. She didn't spot any but, of course, cameras can often be placed in inconspicuous places.

First, Cosette walked around the perimeter of Gabe's land. A pine tree was doing a tango in the breeze. Wands of branches waved in the air. Based on the tree's giant size and the fact that thick moss was carpeting its trunk, Cosette was confident that it was an older tree. As she approached, she spotted an inscription carved into the trunk. It stated, A + G.

I am assuming the G stands for Gabe but who is A? It can't be Patsy, Caprice, Faith, Roseanne, Melissa or Tinsley . Wait a minute, we have never been able to verify that her case is connected but A could stand for Amber Trident. She went missing shortly before the other ladies were killed. I need to visit Nicholas Trident when I am done here and see if his wife knew Gabe.

Next, Cosette passed a shaded rabbit hutch.

It's empty but there were definitely rabbits here at one time. This area is long over due for a cleaning. I don't see anything out of the ordinary, yet.

The detective headed along a leaf lined path toward a grove of trees. Two energetic squirrels scurried away as she approached. A patch of berries lay, mushy and rotting, in the shade, long past their peak. Mushrooms dotted the ground. They reminded Cosette of little sailboats bobbing on the sea.

From the distance, she spotted a sheet of wood along the ground. Approaching, the detective saw that it was covered in splinters. With some effort, Cosette was able to move the wooden plank upward. The swing door groaned and scraped as she opened it. Cement steps, littered with cracks in it, descended into an unknown abyss.

I didn't come this far not to inspect further. We don't have tornadoes or hurricanes in this area. It is highly unusual for someone to have a bunker like this.

Flashing her trusty, and surprisingly bright, phone light, Cosette began to walk down the stairs. She noticed that cobwebs coated the walls but the stairs remained free of them. This indicated to her that someone had been in this basement, on these steps, fairly recently.

Tyler texted Gabe.

You dog! You didn't tell me that you were seeing that hot, new cocktail waitress.

The pool center was particularly quiet during Gabe's shift today so he had been playing Candy Crush on his phone and saw Tyler's text come in instantly.

What are you talking about, dude? I'm not seeing anyone. Why would you think that? There are a few new waitresses at the casino. Who do you even mean?

That super gorgeous one, I think her name is Jenna.

Why would you think I'm seeing her?

I just swung by to see if you were home. I forgot that you were working tonight and, there she was, coming to visit you.

Gabe could feel all the blood draining from his face. He was producing enough stomach acid to burn a hole into a metal bank safe.

There is no way that viper was paying me a friendly visit. Did she figure out that I'm the killer? After all, she worked with Melissa. Did Melissa tell her we were in a secret relationship and that busy body put two and two together? I need to get out of here and get home. I'll pretend that I have a stomach bug and say I need to clock out of work. Then, Miss Jenna will regret the day that she was ever born.

Interrupting his thoughts, Tyler texted again,

Gabe, are you there?

Yes, I'm here. I'm not dating her. I have no clue why she would be at my house.

Fury rose within him. It was a familiar visitor. Gabe's hands trembled and he could feel bile rising up into his parched throat.

Cosette descended into the gloom. The smell of mold and mildew overpowered her senses. She reached the bottom of the stairs and entered a short hallway. A well fed rat skittered along the cement wall past her. From the distance, the detective could hear a rustling sound.

Oh, probably more rats. I hope I can stomach this adventure. I had been feeling queasy even before seeing rodents.

Her glock held at the ready, Cosette proceeded into the ominous depths of the man-made dungeon. She heard a whimper and strained to see a figure in the blackness of the stale smelling room. Approaching the distressed person, she could see that it was a woman heavily wrapped in duct tape and rope.

"Tinsley?" gasped Cosette.

"Oh God, please don't hurt me!" begged the tortured lady.

Cosette knelt at Tinsley's side and began to untie her bindings.

"It's me, Cosette. Please don't be scared. I am here to help you. Let's get you out of these ties."

The young lady was badly bruised and had lost a great deal of weight.

"I can't believe you are here, Cosette. I was sure I was about to die. Gabe came down here once a day, if even that. He'd give me water and a bite of bread. He told me that he wanted my torture to linger. Then he would kill me. He's a monster. Please get me out of here!"

Just then, Cosette heard the distant sound of the swing door above opening. The distinctive groaning and scraping sound sent shivers throughout her body. With her glock in one hand and her taser in the other, she raced to hide behind the entry door of the basement. The killer called out into the darkness.

"Oh, Jenna. I know you are around here somewhere. It would be in your best interest to cooperate with me. People who fail to obey me don't have a very good outcome." The evil man's laughter was deafening.

Gabe's large, intimidating figure passed by the door.

He walked over to Tinsley and noticed that her bindings were partially untied. The serial killer erupted into fitful screams of anger.

Cosette postioned the glock in Gabe's direction and commanded,

"Don't move or I'll shoot and don't think I wont."

"Jenna? You are such a stupid fool. Do you really think that I believe you have the guts to shoot me? And how does a cocktail waitress even know how to use a gun properly?"

"Don't test me, Gabe. I wont hesitate to blow you to pieces if you come closer."

The brutish man grabbed Tinsley by the neck and threatened,

"Your little buddy, here will be history if you don't put that damn gun of yours down!"

Just then, another person stormed into the dungeon. It was Tommy! He raced towards Gabe and threw cuffs on him before he even realized that another person had entered the scene. Moments later, the area was flooded with law enforcement. Gabe had failed to close the basement's swing door after he entered. As a result, Tommy was able to silently approach. The killer was apprehended and taken to the police station. Another monster was no longer on the streets!

47

Tinsley was rushed to the hospital. She was severely dehydrated and weak. Cosette stayed with her during the ride in the ambulance.

I can't believe that this murderer is finally off the streets and Tinsley will survive. I am not sure how much longer she would have lived.

They arrived at the Barton Memorial Hospital. Tinsley requested that Cosette remain with her. She pleaded with the detective to call her beloved Peter. The heartbroken man picked up on the first ring. Cosette had rarely heard such extreme elation.

"My Tinsley is alive? I have been praying day and night for her to be safe. I can't live without her and I also felt so much guilt that I had visited my father the day she was kidnapped. Please let me come and see her right now."

"Of course, she is eager for you to get here. See you soon, Peter."

After Cosette hung up, she felt the room spinning around her. She could see that Tinsley was speaking to her but she couldn't hear the words coming out of her mouth. Her hearing became muffled. The last thing Cosette remembered was that she attempted to brace herself on the edge of the examining table.

The next time she opened her eyes, she was sprawled out on the floor. A concerned looking doctor was kneeling next to her while checking her pulse.

"Ms. DuPont, I am afraid you fainted. Have you had other episodes like this recently?"

"Yes, I have been feeling dizzy and queasy."

"Hmm, perhaps you are dehydrated. Why don't we run some lab tests on you. We can put you in a comfortable bed and give you some fluids until you feel better."

"Oh no, I have so much paperwork to finish up on. I need to get over to the police station."

"Unfortunately, you are in no position to go anywhere. I highly recommend that you rest here for a while. We need to figure out what is going on with you. Can you imagine if you would have had a spell like this while driving?"

"Ok, I know you are right but as soon as I get my results back and feel better, I will really need to go."

"Deal, young lady!"

The kind hearted doctor smiled and arranged for Cosette's tests and a room assignment.

Gabe Patterson's home was stormed. Law enforcement found a collection of stingray skinned wallets and Aquarius pendants in a drawer. There was a large freezer located in his garage. To their horror, a body was discovered. It was Amber Trident! She had a wallet in her grasp and an Aquarius necklace clasped around her bruised neck.

Under a loose board, below his pet snake's terrarium, a box full of photos of each of his victim's corpses and a journal was discovered.

Amber Trident's photos were covered with hearts which Gabe had doodled.

The journal was combed through by law enforcement. Any questions, the police may have had seemed to be answered in Gabe's diary. Sutter Munro had a meeting with a few FBI agents. He briefed them on what he knew about the serial killer so far.

"Seems our killer had a traumatic childhood. He was beaten by his single mother and he started using hard drugs at the age of twelve. Gabe admitted in the journal that he had purposely drowned his younger sister. He enjoyed the act and it left him pining to murder again. However, he held off on killing for years. Gabe used women and threw them away like used napkins. That all changed when he met Amber Trident. According to his words, he fell hopelessly in love with her. She left him standing at the altar, ditched him for another man. That was the straw that broke the camel's back. He figured that if he killed her and put her in his freezer, he could have her for eternity. However, it didn't quench his thirst to murder. Gabe realized that he needed the high, intoxicated feeling he experienced when killing.

That is where our other victims come in. He is close friends with August Winters. He killed Roseanne and Caprice because he wanted to get back at them for hurting his friend. Patsy was just a random woman who caught his attention. Based on what he wrote, nobody, including August, had any idea he was killing. Nobody that is, except for Melissa. He killed her because she knew too much.

The items he left with the victims are significant because Amber Trident is an Aquarius. He gifted her an Aquarius pendant while they were together. Amber gave him a stingray skin wallet during their engagement. Gabe also gifted his friend Tyler that type of a wallet. That is why Cosette saw him with one at the bike-a-thon. Gabe was planning on killing Tinsley within the week. After Tinsley, his next victim would have been our Cosette DuPont. He is obsessed with the recent Virginia City serial killer. Gabe wanted to help him finish the job of slaying Cosette. We found this beast just in the nick of time. Ms. DuPont deserves tremendous accolades. She cracked this difficult case wide open."

Cosette was in a light sleep when she heard her hospital room door open. It was Luke.

"Oh, Luke, I am so happy to see you."

"Baby, do you think I could ever stay away? I heard what happened. Are you ok? I have been worried sick."

"Yes, sweetheart, I am fine."

"I am so proud of you. I heard you caught that wretched killer. Do you realize that you gave a lot of families closure and you saved potential future victims of his? If you weren't injured, why are you in a hospital bed though?"

"It is no big deal, Luke. I promise. I felt dizzy and fainted but it was just for a few minutes."

"You fainted? What? Why? That isn't like you."

"It is probably just from exhaustion and dehydration."

Just then, a quiet knock sounded at the door.

Cosette called, "Come in please."

It was Dr. Lambert, the physician who had ordered lab work for her.

When the slender, salt and pepper haired doctor noticed that Cosette was not alone, he offered to return at another time.

"No, please, come in, Doctor. This is my fiancé, Luke Meier. There isn't anything he can't hear."

"If you are sure…Ok, the lab results have returned. Your EKG was perfect. Your blood count and glucose levels are fine as well. I decided to run a serum pregnancy test. It came back positive. You are expecting and based on your hCG count, you are about ten weeks along."

Cosette and Luke both gasped.

"How is this possible?" inquired Cosette. "I am on the Pill."

"When taken correctly, the Pill is around 99% effective. Have you had antibiotics in the last few months? They can reduce the pills efficiency."

"Yes, I had a sinus infection about three months ago. I was on a course of antibiotics."

Although, the couple had not planned to expand their family until after the wedding in April, they were both very happy. Their eyes sparkled and their face muscles hurt from smiling so severely.

Dr. Lambert continued, "I would recommend discontinuing the Pill immediately. Let's set you up for an ultrasound to confirm the due date."

The gentle doctor peered at the hospital's schedule. Dr. Jardain is our top obstetrician. Could you see him for a prenatal appointment this coming Tuesday at 10:00 a.m? At that point, he can do an exam and ultrasound."

"I"ll clear my schedule," beamed Luke.

"I wouldn't miss it! Spencer is going to be so excited to hear the incredible news!" replied the expectant mother.

Tinsley awoke to her beloved Peter standing next to her. He gently sat on the edge of her bed and embraced her. They both began to cry.

"Tinsley, I never thought I would see you again. I basically died the day you went missing, just going through the motions of life like a zombie. I also felt so guilty for letting you out of my sight and visiting my dad without you. I was a fool! Please forgive me, baby?"

"Peter, there is nothing to forgive. You're the best boyfriend on earth. I can't tell you how much I missed you. I never thought I would be in your arms again. I'm pretty sure that monster was about to kill me."

"I will never let anyone hurt you again, Tinsley."

Peter stood and rummaged in the pocket of his trousers.

"This is really not the way I envisioned doing this. I pictured doing this on a beach at sunset or on a mountain top. There is one thing I've learned since you went missing. Every single second of life is precious. You never know when it will all end. Cherish the ones you love."

Peter bent down onto one knee and opened the ring box. It was a stunning, princess cut engagement ring. Tinsley felt like she was dreaming.

"Tinsley, will you give me the great honor of becoming my wife? I promise to love and cherish you forever."

"Oh, yes, Peter! A million times over, yes! I feel like spending eternity with you is not even long enough."

Epilogue

"B'sheym heyley benshakhar, b'sheym hassatan. In the name of the Shining One, Son of the Morning. In the name of Satan."

Chants rose into the hot, summer night air like helium balloons escaping their confines. The cult members raised their arms while calling out in unison, "Hail Satan!"

A makeshift altar had been set up in a grove of Redwood Trees. The members appeared to be in a trance-like state. Standing in a crescent moon shaped configuration, they were all dressed in black. An exceptionally tall, strongly built figure, cloaked in a black robe, led the ceremony. Candles perched on top of the altar, illuminated his outline. After the ceremony concluded, the leader, Abaddon, announced updates to the members of the cult.

"I am not liking our numbers at all. We haven't added new members in some time. I understand that living in the small town of Deal, limits how many newcomers we can find. However, we have got to step our efforts up. We need to thrive and ultimately become the rulers of the world. Let's mainly focus on recruitment right now. Also, sacrificing Belle London was foolish. She was way too high profile of a person. Slaying the homecoming queen of Deal High was just plain stupid. Cops are asking a lot of questions. From now on, our sacrifices need to focus on people who will not be missed such as runaways, rudderless teens and drifters.

Abaddon adjourned the meeting and the Satanists silently drifted off into the undergrowth of the dense forest.

Winter Wells sprung up from her desk as the final bell at Linden High School rang. She exited the building feeling a combination of excitement and nostalgia. Her long, wavy, caramel colored hair bounced along her back. Winters' crystal blue eyes blinked away the intense, afternoon sunlight.

She had just finished her junior year. It was finally summer vacation. The beautiful, fun loving teen had lived in Linden, New Jersey her entire life. Recently, her minister father received a job offer he could not refuse. Mr. Wells was hired to be the lead minister in a church in Deal, Nevada. Unlike his current job, he would now also hold a supervisory role.

I am so proud of Dad but I still can't believe we are moving as far away as Nevada. That is clear across the country. Most of my friends here, I have known since pre school. I will miss them a lot but, at least, there is always FaceTime. Besides, who knows, I could end up having many interesting adventures there.

To my son, Jason, for his tireless devotion to editing, cover design and technical assistance.

To my sister, Andrea Hofstadter, and to my brother, Christian Hofstadter, for being an incredible support to me, not just when I am writing a novel, but always.

To my daughter, Olivia, who was the model for this book cover.

To my sister, Katherine Hlavac, and my brother, Robert Hlavac, for encouraging and supporting my writing endeavors.

To my other family members; Mark, Lauren, Sara, and my mother, Astrid, for always believing in me and guiding me.

Liquid Deceptions would not have been possible without the love and kindness from all of you.

Liquid Deceptions

See more at:
www.colleenhlavac.com